I0556172

LYDIA

Servant Siblings Series: Book 5

JENIFER JENNINGS

Copyright © 2024 Jenifer Jennings

All rights reserved. Except as permitted under the U.S. Copyright Act of 1976, no part of this book may be reproduced or transmitted in any form or by any means, electronic or mechanical, including photocopying and recording, or by an information storage and retrieval system, without permission in writing from the publisher.

Editor: Jill Monday

Scripture quotations and paraphrases are taken from The Holy Bible, English Standard Version, Copyright © 2001 by Crossway, a publishing ministry of Good News Publishers.

This book is a work of historical fiction based closely on real people and events recorded in the Holy Bible. Details that cannot be historically verified are purely products of the author's imagination. Any resemblance to actual persons, living or dead, or actual events is purely coincidental.

ISBN: 978-1-954105-32-4

For Aurora, I pray God reveals Himself to you in wonderful ways.

"And the word of God continued to increase, and the number of the disciples multiplied greatly in Jerusalem, and a great many of the priests became obedient to the faith. And Stephen, full of grace and power, was doing great wonders and signs among the people."

-Acts 6:7-8

CHAPTER 1

33 A.D., Jerusalem

Lydia pushed her long braid over her shoulder and grabbed a pail on her way outside.

"Shalom, Michal," she greeted the female goat.

The animal barely glanced in her direction as it continued grazing on weeds in the open courtyard.

Squatting low, Lydia placed the pail under the goat, pushed up the sleeves of her tunic, and set to milking.

As the ivory liquid filled the container, Lydia hummed to herself. "You've got it pretty good here in the villa, Michal. I mean, as far as a goat's life can get.

You keep producing milk and Theodotos will keep you around. Not like those others he slaughters in the Temple every day."

She surveyed the other animals as her hands fell into a rhythmic pace. "You don't have to worry about a bunch of siblings bossing you around either. Me, on the other hand? My older brothers, James and Joseph, act like Jerusalem's walls would fall if they weren't in charge. Assia is tucked away in the boring town of Nazareth, living out her dream of being a wife. And Jude spends all his time with his nose in scrolls or gesturing with his deaf betrothed."

The male goat strolled over to Lydia and butted her with his head.

"I'm busy, Daniel." She nudged the goat away with her elbow. "I'll bring you some scraps later."

Daniel buried his face in the weeds beside Michal.

Lydia sighed. "And where's Simon, the brother I'm normally responsible for? He had the good sense to disappear months ago. Though, I might as well have run away with him for as much as anyone pays attention to me."

A loud crowing pierced the air around Lydia.

"Thank you, Enoch," she called up to the rooster perched nearby. "But you're too late for this household. My mother makes it her aim to be up before your cries. Her daughters are not afforded the luxury of waiting for you either. Too much to do."

As Michal's flow decreased, Lydia wiped away the small beads of sweat forming on her brow. "I know I should be grateful. At least James had the sense not to force me back to Nazareth with Assia. I don't miss that dusty little town in the slightest. Jerusalem has much more to offer."

She rose and stretched her back. "Besides, I'm sure Assia got pregnant the instant she became Hiskiel's bride. I wouldn't have been able to take her flaunting a growing belly in my face every day. It's bad enough that Elissa's midsection is swollen with life. At least she has the decency not to force herself to be the center of attention."

Picking up the pail, she noticed the weight was off. "Hmm, you're a lot lighter today." She swirled the liquid. "Oh, Michal, don't tell me you're pregnant, too."

Michal ruminated on the bits of vegetation poking out the sides of her mouth, oblivious to the accusation.

"Terrific." She blew away some strands of hair that had fallen into her face and moved to the other female goat. "Shalom, Abigail." She set the pail under the animal. "I'm sure you'll be faithful with your supply today."

She warmed her hands and set to work. "I'm not sure who's worse, my three overbearing brothers or my lazy younger sister, Salome. Poor girl has her head stuck in the clouds waiting for our oldest brother to come back down." She flicked her gaze to the gray sky. "No one has the heart to tell her he's not coming back anytime soon."

A gentle nudge to her back caused her to turn.

The white colt stood behind her, his large eyes almost pleading.

"Shalom, Boaz." She reached out and rubbed his soft muzzle.

Boaz closed his eyes and leaned into her strokes.

Visions of palm branches and praises flooded her mind. *Jesus.* Her oldest brother's name echoed through her as a half-question, half-prayer.

She huffed some hair away from her face. "Of course He turned out to be Messiah. He's perfect. Just like everyone else in this family. Except me," she paused, "and maybe Simon." She continued milking Abigail. "But where is Jesus? Gone. Just like Assia and Simon. And I'm stuck here with the rest of them. But do they care about me?"

"Baa," Abigail answered.

"That's right. They sure don't. It's 'Lydia, do this' and 'Lydia, do that.' I'm often treated more like a servant than a sister. Some days, I wish I could disappear."

"Maa."

"You're right." She sighed. "They'd be lost without me. Who would do their work for them while they run around Jerusalem, taking care of every Moses and Miriam with their hands out?"

When Abigail was sufficiently milked, Lydia headed back toward the house. A wind picked up, causing her dress to flutter and the skin of her exposed arms to prickle.

She shivered. "The rainy season is certainly upon us." She pushed down her sleeves and looked at Michal. "Another reason for you to be grateful. No matter how cold it gets, you'll be taken care of here."

She let her gaze drift toward the streets. "Unlike so many others."

She scratched the place behind Michal's left ear she knew was the goat's favorite. "I'm sure Theodotus will be pleased with your news. I'll inform him this evening."

Retreating inside the villa, she deposited the pail beside her mother in the kitchen, kissed her cheek, and moved to warm her hands beside the continual fire.

Mary arranged bowls onto a platter. "Lydia, would you bring these to the men?"

I can't even have a moment to warm myself. "Yes, Ima." Lydia collected the tray and left to deliver it to the men waiting to break their fast.

Jesus' collection of disciples had grown to include an additional seven who'd been tasked with meeting the needs of the Hellenistic widows in Jerusalem. These men often arrived with the sun, seeking wisdom from James and Peter before heading out for the day.

Lydia wove herself through the throng of men to deposit the platter on the low table. She knew the dishes would be empty before she had a chance to return to the kitchen, so she waited. It was an easy excuse for a reprieve from her chores.

The hum of voices sounded like a hive with news being brought in and orders being handed out. Each man assigned tasks, which all seemed very much the same to her. Exchange coins for food and clothing, patch a roof, check on the sick and dying. The men's chores blended with her own. Milk the goats, wash the dishes, prepare the food. Task after task, day after day.

Only to lay her head down and wake to the same tasks waiting the next day.

She sighed to herself as she watched the dishes empty and moved to retrieve the platter.

A man reached for the last dried fig, but bumped into her arm instead. "Forgive me." He withdrew his hand. "I thought I saw…" He pointed to the fig.

"Oh." Lydia plucked the shriveled fruit from the bowl and held it out. "I thought my brothers had devoured everything."

"Brothers?" He accepted the fig and eyed the gathering. "Which ones are your brothers?"

She pointed to a semi-circle of four men. "Those three there, but not the fisherman."

"Ah." He nodded. "The fisherman is Peter, right?"

"He answers to Simon Peter sometimes." She gestured to each of her brothers. "James, Joseph, and Jude. Three of my older brothers."

"I see the resemblance."

Lydia's lips twisted.

"Not that you look like a man," he quickly added, twisting the stem of the fig between his fingers. "What I meant was that you look like your brothers, but in a different way."

She scrunched her forehead.

"Forgive me." He rubbed the back of his neck. "I've made a mess of the compliment. Can we start over?" He dipped his head. "I'm called Stephen."

Lydia held her guard for a few moments longer until she noticed red crawling up his neck and softened. "You can call me Lydia."

"Lydia," Stephen repeated. "A fitting name." He smiled so wide it squinted his eyes.

Before she could ask his meaning, Joseph stepped nearer.

"The others are heading out, Stephen." Joseph glanced at his sister. "Peter wants everyone to try to stay ahead of the storm coming in, and we've got extra tasks getting everyone ready before Shabbat."

Lydia nodded. "I'll make sure Ima has warm bread and stew ready when you return."

Stephen kept his attention on Lydia.

Joseph cleared his throat.

"Oh." Stephen shook his head. "Your sister was introducing herself."

"Don't get too attached to her," Joseph teased. "Lydia enjoys spending more of her time with animals rather than people."

"At least they don't protest when I speak," Lydia defended. "Unlike most of my siblings."

Stephen chuckled.

Joseph lifted an eyebrow at her. "Don't you have chores waiting?"

"Don't you have widows waiting?" Lydia fired a verbal arrow back at her brother.

"Yes, *we* do." He motioned between himself and Stephen.

Lydia picked up the empty platter from the table. "You should get to it then."

Joseph shook his head and turned away.

Stephen moved to give Lydia room to leave. "Don't take his words to heart."

She caught his bright eyes. Staring into them for too long, she noticed they were a strange color; like ginger tea that had been left to steep too long.

Stephen lifted a shoulder. "It's simply a brother thing." He tossed the fig into his mouth and chewed it vigorously.

She blinked several times, untying her gaze from his. "I know all too well." She moved past him. "I've got five of them and two sisters."

"I have five brothers as well. All older than I."

"Then you know what it's like too."

He nodded slowly. "It would have been nice to have a sister, though."

She searched his down-turned face.

"I would have probably learned how to act more appropriately around women."

Despite herself, Lydia allowed a smile to crease her lips. "You're not so bad at it."

"I—"

"Let's go, Stephen," Joseph called from the other side of the room.

Stephen lifted an embarrassed expression.

"Go on." She flicked her head. "My brothers don't like to be kept waiting."

"It was a pleasure meeting you, Lydia." He bowed and hurried after the group, departing for the day.

"And you, Stephen," she whispered to herself.

CHAPTER 2

The hours passed too quickly for Lydia as she hurried from one chore to another. Preparing for Shabbat meant shoving two days' worth of work into one.

While the house servants, Zipporah and Ria, knew well how to prepare a villa for the day of rest, they became overwhelmed when the house was overtaken by Jesus' followers. Even Moges, the steward of the household, often ventured into the city with the men instead of staying to attend to the daily chores.

I'm always racing the sun, Lydia thought to herself as she bustled around the kitchen. *Everything must be done before the sun sets or it will have to wait another day.*

Elissa moved slower around the spacious room and often let soft grunts escape while attempting her tasks.

Lydia caught her sister-in-law's frustration as her swollen belly prevented her from getting as close to things as she once could.

"Give yourself grace," Mary encouraged. "Your body is growing new life."

Elissa took a deep breath and adjusted herself to reach over the table.

Lydia endured hours of her mother fussing over Elissa. She wondered if the older woman was making up for not being in Nazareth tending to her own daughter's growing family.

Pretty soon Elissa will be completely spared from her chores while she tends to a newborn. Lydia caught herself staring at her sister-in-law's large stomach and shook her attention away.

Mary poured oil into a lamp. "We need to purchase more oil." She allowed the last few drops to drip into the clay vessel.

Lydia nodded a simple agreement. *We'd have more if James and Peter didn't insist on spreading Theodotus' wealth around Jerusalem.*

The priest had been more than generous to the family and the followers, but Lydia felt the men often pressed the limits of the man's open hands.

"We ration everything as far as we can." Lydia scrubbed a stone cup. "I fear James will ask us to sacrifice even more as we endure the chill of the winter rains."

"Adonai has always provided for this family and His people," Mary reminded her. "There is no reason to start doubting Him now."

"You're the one who taught us how to ration." Lydia dropped the cup into the water. "Where Jude sees papyrus for scrolls, I see ropes, baskets, and even wound treatment. Where James sees oil for lamps, I see soap, cooking oil, and fly repellent. Ima, we know well how to survive on little, but we can't possibly care for the needs of every empty hand and stomach in Jerusalem."

Mary moved toward Lydia and cupped her cheeks. "Adonai will provide." She kissed her forehead and released her hold. "Salome and Arava should be back from the stream soon with clean clothes. Then we will be ready for Shabbat." She moved to help Elissa.

Lydia stared down at the murky water. "Does James have to continue to test even Adonai's limits?"

She finished the dishes and moved to check the kitchen for others that needed a good scrub. As she went, she collected every scrap unworthy for the human residents of the villa. She deposited them in the folds of her tunic for those who took up residence in the outer courtyard.

Finding a few moments before the men were expected to return, Lydia stole away outside.

Two chickens plucked at the ground behind her, seeking insects stirred by her steps. The goats meandered around the space, searching for anything edible.

"Here." Lydia reached into her dress and produced a handful of morsels. She held them out to Daniel. "I promised I'd bring you something."

The male goat eagerly accepted the delicacies.

Lydia brushed the crumbs onto the ground for the chickens who fluttered to partake of the bits. She moved toward the wooden overhang that provided shade and protection for the animals.

Theodotus' female donkey, Judith, stood underneath with her white colt.

Lydia approached the mother with an apple core. "I saved this for you."

Judith's lips enclosed around the gift, and it crunched loudly as she chewed.

Boaz nuzzled against Lydia.

Rubbing his long muzzle, Lydia inhaled the quiet moment into her soul. Her day had been filled with noise and hurry. To simply pause and soak in the refreshment that she found spending time with the animals was a balm to her spirit. No human had ever afforded her such peace.

"Kraa."

Lydia turned toward the sound to find a raven perched on the wooden railing of the overhang.

"Shalom, friend." She bowed her head toward the bird. "I haven't seen you around here before."

"Kraa-kraa." The bird bounced along the rail.

"Let's see." Lydia dug into the folds of her tunic. "I think I might have something in here." She searched for anything remaining. "Ah." Lifting her hand, she produced a few almonds. "I was saving these for myself, but you can have them." She held the tiny nuts out toward the bird.

With a flutter of black wings, the raven snatched the almonds from her hands and swallowed them whole before Lydia had a chance to blink.

"My, you are hungry." She examined the raven. "You've got such interesting markings. Your body is gray, but your head, wings, and tail feathers are black. It's as if Adonai started painting you, but you flew away before He could finish."

"Kraa."

"I'm sorry, I haven't got anything else." She held up her empty hands.

The bird tilted its head to one side and then the

other as if searching for something.

"I don't know if the priest would like you hanging around here. Adonai has marked you unclean." She moved closer. "They even put spikes on the Temple roof to keep your kind from feasting on the sacrifices."

She curled one finger and stroked the bird's chest with her knuckle. "Though I don't think an animal should have any less worth simply because they can't be eaten or burned on the altar."

She continued with gentle strokes, encouraged by the bird's low warbling. "You know, my people have a story about your kind. Would you like to hear it?"

"Kraa-kraa."

"There was this prophet named Elijah who was hiding from a wicked king. Adonai showed him a place near a brook where he would be safe. While he was there, Adonai sent a flock of ravens to bring him bread and meat twice a day, every day until the stream dried up. Those birds, deemed unclean, kept the prophet alive."

The raven clicked several times.

"If you decide to stay around, Elijah, keep away from Theodotus." She gave the raven a last stroke. "I've got to get back inside before my mother comes looking for me."

Elijah stretched his long, black wings and took off into the sky.

Lydia made her way into the villa, being sure to give Michal a scratch before leaving the courtyard.

The disciples, along with her brothers, returned to the villa tired and hungry. Their slumped shoulders and dragging feet revealed their long day providing for the needy.

As promised, Mary supplied stew and bread to warm their chilled bodies and stomachs.

While they ate, the men chatted among themselves, eager to share stories.

"The needs are mounting," Peter recounted to James. "It seems every day our list of visits grows."

"We are doing our best with what we have," James answered. "We will simply pray and keep doing what we can."

Lydia refilled cups with watered wine as she listened to bits and pieces of the conversations.

Salome cleared empty dishes and returned with full ones.

"This winter will be a cold one," Peter continued. "I can feel it in my bones. Some of these widows might freeze or starve."

James took a slow sip from his stone cup. "Even with the extra seven men, we don't have enough hands to lift every burden in Jerusalem."

"Why not get more hands?" The question came from Salome.

Every man at the low table turned to her, including Lydia, who held an empty cup to the pitcher in her hand.

"Adonai has called seven to this service," James answered plainly. "I don't know if He will call more."

Salome chewed on her lips as if she were considering whether or not to speak.

"Do you have something else, young one?" James

encouraged her.

"Most of our family is here." Salome waved to Lydia and then her brothers. "But the disciples' families are still back in Galilee. Why not call them here?"

James glanced at Peter. "Do you think they'd come?"

Peter lifted a shoulder. "I don't see why not." He turned to Salome. "But it might be too dangerous to travel during the winter rains."

"Well," Salome set to chewing her bottom lip again, "they could come for Passover. It's only a few months away. We can send word to them now so they can prepare, and then they can leave with the caravans heading here for the feasts."

"We can also send word to any willing to relocate to sell what they can and bring the funds with them," Jude added. He shook his head as he looked around at the other men. "I don't know how many of your families would make such a sacrifice, but we'd be grateful for any who would."

James smiled at Salome over the hushed conversations sparked by the proposals. "Brilliant idea, sister."

Lydia watched her younger sister blush under his praise.

"I'll go to Galilee," Joseph offered.

"You've only just returned from Nazareth," James reminded him.

"Exactly." Joseph held up an open hand. "I already know the journey and can help lead the return."

"Well," James looked around, "it seems we have a plan." His eyes fell on Lydia.

She flinched under his glare. It appeared he was seeking for her to contribute to the arrangements, but she had nothing to offer. Why had she not been the one to have the brilliant ideas?

She ducked away from his gaze. *At least we shall soon have more hands to lighten our loads.*

CHAPTER 3

Shabbat came and went for Lydia while her workload mounted. In exchange, the first day of the week held promise as the market reopened and daily life returned to its traditional pace.

"Please?" Lydia pleaded with James. "I haven't been to the market in ages. I truly wish to go."

James glanced around her to the group waiting for him. "We're going to make visits when we're done at the market. You'll have no one to escort you back to the villa."

She eyed the steward. "What about Moges?"

James shook his head. "Moges has been a great help to us."

"His first duty is to the house of Theodotus."

"We know that, and so does he." James turned soft eyes on Lydia. "Moges is still new to our beliefs. It's been good for him to serve alongside us."

"While we take on his tasks," she muttered under her breath.

James lifted a dark eyebrow at her.

Lydia huffed. "What if Ria comes along? I'm sure there are items that need to be purchased for the household. You said it yourself; the men plan on going into the city afterward." Her shoulders lifted with the confidence of her logic. "Ria and I could join you and bring back the supplies for the villa. That would free the men to make their visits."

After a few moments of silent deliberation, James conceded. "You make a good point. Fetch Ria, and you may join us this morning."

Lydia squealed.

"But the two of you are to return to the villa after we finish our purchases."

She nodded in vigorous agreement and rushed to find the house servant.

Ria was sweeping in the front part of the house.

"Ria!" Lydia shouted as she approached the servant. "Set down your task and follow me."

"Why?" She continued sweeping.

"We are going to the market."

She hesitated. "I thought the men were going today."

"We're joining them." Lydia's smile spread across her face.

"I don't know." Ria began sweeping again. "I've got so much to catch up on."

"I promise," Lydia grabbed the broom, "your tasks will still be waiting for you upon our return." She leaned the slender stick against the wall. "How many times do you get to go to the market?"

Ria put a finger to her chin. "I suppose it wouldn't hurt to go out for a little while."

"Hurry." Lydia moved toward the door. "The men are waiting for us."

Stepping out into the dim light of a chilly day, Lydia pulled her headscarf up to trap heat against her head and ears. Though the gray sky warned of coming rain, the fresh air and call of a market full of undiscovered treasures beckoned her.

Lydia and Ria kept to the back of the men as they ventured through Jerusalem's Upper City.

Some of the large limestone houses were yellow from decades of wind and sun, while others were white with fresh wash. Narrow dirt streets cut between the villas and sloped downward toward the Tyropean Valley. Two arched passageways traversed the valley and reached toward the Temple, wrapping around the Upper City like a guard. They mirrored the thick, gray wall that encircled the entire city.

As they neared the towering passageway, the familiar sound of rushing water greeted them. The aqueduct atop the structure flowed continually with fresh water from the western mountains. Nearing the Temple, the sounds of songs and prayers mixed with the distinct smell of burning animal sacrifices and the special incense mixture used exclusively by the priests.

"Remind me to purchase oil." Lydia led Ria through an arch into the lower city. "I almost forgot Ima said we were low."

"Your mother asked for more material as well."

Lydia rolled her eyes. "She's making an entire chest full of clothes for a child who isn't even here yet."

"What have you got against an unborn child?"

"Nothing." Lydia sighed. "I never had a new garment." She lifted her ill-fitted tunic. "All my clothes passed through Assia's hands first." She dropped her garment back into place. "It would be nice to own one dress that was mine first."

"Think of poor Salome."

"Oh, yes, poor Salome." Lydia clicked her tongue in frustration. "She has never cared about her clothes. She probably would have worn our brothers' work tunics as a little girl if Ima had let her. The silly thing cared more for running about and climbing trees than anything else."

On the other side of the arches, the buildings grew small and compacted. Among them ran a long market street, containing booths that provided sustenance for the residents and visitors of Jerusalem. The street, which was only quiet on Shabbat, was very much alive with the sounds of craftsmen and shouts of sellers on the first day of the week. The clatter of hooves competed with the clang of metalworkers' tools along the road.

Varying tradesmen had organized themselves into groups long ago, clustered together in sections of the lower city like grapes. Many of them added a synagogue in their sector for their workers to attend. This tradition led to hundreds of synagogues in the city.

Passing the pottery booths, Lydia hesitated briefly at one. "Shalom, Benjamin."

The old potter smiled as he molded the clay upon his wheel. "How's my daughter?"

Lydia tried not to take his lack of interest in her wellbeing to heart. After all, he was not her father. "Elissa is well and will set a child upon your knee soon."

"I will be glad of that day."

Lydia rubbed the side of a finished water pot, admiring the delicate details of the craftsman's hands. "You should join us next Shabbat."

The wrinkles on Benjamin's face deepened. "I accept the offer."

"Until then." She bowed and caught up to the men.

Lydia fluttered from one side of the market street to the other like a bee collecting honey from a field of wildflowers. The colors, sights, and smells held such wonder for her.

She aided Ria in selecting fruits, vegetables, dried fish, and oil.

Once their bags were full, Lydia took a few moments to linger at a nearby perfume booth, sampling the smells of far-off places and enticing mixes created to delight the senses.

Warming a small bottle in her hands, she lifted the vessel to her nose and inhaled. Through the wax seal, the spicy, sweet perfume of spikenard tickled her nostrils.

Returning the precious substance to its owner, she caught sight of a familiar woman passing through the street with a collection of followers. She kept her eyes on the woman who lingered at a booth of precious stones and jewelry.

Ria came around the edge of the perfume booth. "Who's that?"

"Penelope," Lydia answered without removing her gaze from the woman. "She's recently betrothed to Saul of Tarsus."

"She's rather beautiful."

"Yes." Lydia observed the perfect lines of the girl across the way. "Some women have all the fortune." She glanced sideways at Ria. "Of course, life must be easier when you are born into a wealthy family and handed everything your heart desires." She allowed her gaze to drift back to Penelope. "Unlike the rest of us, who have to work hard for every scrap."

The crowd shifted, allowing Lydia to catch sight of Saul.

He deposited coins into the hands of the seller for the selections of his betrothed.

"That's Saul?" Ria asked Lydia.

"That's him."

"Uh."

Lydia turned to face the younger girl. "What?"

"From Jude's descriptions, I imagined him to be rather…" She twisted her hand in the air, searching for an appropriate description.

"Unpleasant?"

"To say the least." She waved toward the couple. "Jude speaks of the man as if he's a slobbering jackal. When, in fact, he's merely a man." She set her hand on her hip. "A short, unimposing man at that."

"Don't be fooled." Lydia smirked. "Vipers often hide and strike when you least expect it."

"I shall be sure to give him a wide berth, then." Ria moved toward the next booth. "What kind of material should we bring back for Mary?"

Lydia's gaze lingered a few more moments on Saul and Penelope. Her heart ached with a longing she couldn't put into words.

"Lydia?"

Ria's voice snatched her attention. "Forgive me. What did you ask?"

She pointed to a stack of material. "For your mother."

"Right." Lydia inspected the selections. "We don't have to worry about warmth right now, as Elissa won't give birth until the weather turns." She rubbed at a woven cloth. "Something more like this." She held up the piece. "What do you think?"

"It looks sturdy."

"Yes." Lydia examined the cloth further. "We want material that will last."

Ria bartered with the seller until they came to an agreement. She retrieved the coins given to her by Mary and handed them to the woman. "I'm sure your mother will be pleased."

It takes much more to please my mother. Lydia kept the thought private.

Indulging the last few moments of precious freedom, Lydia allowed her fingers to graze the dresses. She sighed to herself.

"Any good selections?"

An unexpected voice startled Lydia. She turned and came face to face with Saul. His sly smile set the hairs on her neck on edge. She looked around and found Ria had moved on and her brother was nowhere in sight. She wondered if it was favor or folly that she was this close to the snake alone.

Saul perused the piles. "Penelope?"

The beautiful woman floated closer to them and allowed her gaze to graze the materials. "These are a bit too plain for my taste."

"You're right." Saul slid his eyes in Lydia's direction. "Much too plain."

Heat rose on the sides of Lydia's neck, and she clenched her jaw. As much as she wanted to let a few choice words fly in Saul's direction, she knew better than to pick a fight with a viper. She might win, but she'd risk being bitten in the process.

"Say, Lydia, how's Jude doing in his studies?" He lifted one eyebrow. "I wonder if he's heard the good news. I'm going to take my seat among the Pharisees soon."

Lydia's jaw flinched. She fought harder to keep her lips sealed.

"Is her brother going to be on the council too?" Penelope asked.

"No." Saul shook his head. "Their family is from Nazareth." His smile slithered sideways. "Nothing good ever comes out of Nazareth."

Something inside Lydia snapped. "You filthy—"

"Whoa!" A man stepped between her and Saul.

Lydia didn't recognize the back of the person until she heard him speak.

"There's no need for such talk." Stephen held up his hands toward Saul.

Lydia clamped her mouth shut, but the heat still burned the sides of her neck.

CHAPTER 4

Watching Saul slink away like a dog with his tail between his legs, Lydia held back the surge of emotions churning inside. Relief that Saul had been sent away. Anger that he'd gotten away with his words. Embarrassment that Stephen had to step in between them.

As if hearing her warring thoughts, Stephen turned to face her. "Are you well?"

Lydia furrowed her brow, unsure of the intent of his question.

"Did he harm you?"

She shook her head; both at his question and to shake off her confusion. "No."

The relief that washed off him was palatable. His shoulders drooped and he let out a heavy sigh. "Good."

"Thank you," she squeaked out over her turmoil.

The corners of Stephen's mouth raised. "I'm sorry to be of service, but I'm glad to have been nearby."

Despite her rapid heartbeat and tight throat, she returned a small smile.

Stephen's attention drifted to the booth. "Doing some shopping?"

She held up her full bags. "For the villa and some material for my mother."

"James shared about his good news." Stephen ran

his hands over a selection of fabric. "He's looking forward to being an abba."

"I'm sure he is." Her attention dropped to her sandals.

"Which one is your favorite?"

Lydia's attention jumped up to meet his. "What?"

"Which one do you like?" He pointed to a stack of dresses. "I saw you admiring them."

"Oh, they're all beautiful." She took a step backward. "I've never owned a new dress before." She lifted her worn tunic. "Always ones from my sister and mother."

"Well," he patted the pile, "which one do you like?"

She shook her head. "I can't afford such luxury." She took another step back, this time to give herself a clearer view of the market street as she searched for Ria and James. "I really should get back to the villa."

"I'm sure you have much to do." He let his hand drop to his side. "I should probably find the others before they leave the market." He bowed his head toward Lydia. "A pleasure, as always."

She dipped her head. "My thanks again."

Stephen merged into the crowd.

"There you are." Ria walked up to Lydia. "I thought you were behind me this whole time, and I turned and you were gone."

Lydia kept her eyes on the place where Stephen disappeared.

"Lydia, you look unwell."

"A bit shaken," she admitted. "I had an encounter

with a viper."

"Oh, my." Ria's hands flew to her mouth. "Did it bite you?"

"No." Lydia smiled to herself. "I was rescued from its venom."

"Do tell."

"On our way to the villa." She adjusted the strap across her body. "We need to get back."

Lydia shared her encounter with Saul and his spiteful words and Stephen's interjection as they followed the winding streets to Theodotus' house.

Ria hung on her every word. "That Stephen is certainly a good man," she gave her estimation as they neared the villa.

"Yes." Lydia's thoughts drifted to Stephen's ginger eyes. "He certainly is."

"How is your sister-in-law?" Ria shifted topics.

"As well as a pregnant woman can be."

"It must be a strain on one's body to grow a new life."

"I suppose." Lydia lifted a shoulder. "Though it often puts a strain on everyone else as well."

"What do you mean?"

"I mean, my workload has increased," Lydia confided in her. "Elissa can't do her full workload, so who do you think lifts the lack? Me."

"I'm sure she would stand in the gap if it were you."

Lydia let out a sigh. "I know she would." She put her hand on the large wooden door of the villa. "I'm surrounded by pregnant beings. Even the goat is pregnant." She waved her hand toward the outer courtyard. "I'm sure my older sister will arrive pregnant as well." She pushed the door open. "This is my mother's dream and my nightmare."

"No one is pregnant forever," Ria reminded her.

Lydia wiped her face. "Thank Adonai for that."

On the other side of the door, they parted ways.

Ria returned to her sweeping, while Lydia took their purchases to the kitchen.

Elissa sat in a corner, fanning herself with a cloth. She rose at Lydia's entrance to inspect the haul. "Did you find any citrons?"

Lydia shook her head. "It's too early for citrus."

"I know." Elissa hung her head. "But they're all I've been thinking about today."

Mary set aside her kneading. "Your body is craving what it needs." She searched through the items. "I'll find you something to satisfy the desire."

Lydia unloaded the satchels and retrieved the material. "Here you are, Ima." She held up a length of sturdy linen.

Reaching out, Mary inspected the material. "Perfect." She folded the fabric. "Once we put these away, I need you to start with more food preparations."

"More?"

"Theodotus sent word after you left that he has invited several priests to the evening meal." She waved around the room. "Elissa has been doing her best. Arava and I are making some fresh loaves. Salome is retrieving more water. Zipporah and Ria have been instructed to prepare the house while we prepare the food."

There are always more mouths to feed. Lydia sighed to herself as she emptied the last bag. *I wonder if Jesus considered who would feed them when he told us to make disciples.*

She sharpened a knife and set to work slicing the long, dark radishes she discovered in the market. They were popular this time of year and she had her pick of some rather large ones. Their dark brown skins were fresh, allowing them to be left on to be consumed with the white interior.

For Lydia, meal preparations had become as effortless as breathing. Time-consuming, but effortless. She kneaded dough, built fires, collected water, and tended to young ones all her life. She'd held a blade since she could walk and was milking goats by the time she could reach their udders.

With the steady motion of her hands on the borrowed blade, her mind was free to wander. It often wandered to stories or hopes of seeing the world beyond her station. Today, her mind traveled to the bright eyes and handsome smile of Stephen. She knew she shouldn't allow her thoughts to dwell on a man who was not hers, but she couldn't resist. He'd shown her such kindness and compassion in their few encounters. Even with the limited interactions, she could fully understand why he'd been chosen to help with the needs of the widows and the fatherless. He was a man filled with the attributes of Adonai.

The women piled dishes and platters with food, cleaned the entire house, and prepared tables to welcome the guests of Theodotus.

As evening fell over the city, priests filled the villa and settled in to enjoy the well-prepared meal.

Lydia opted to help serve so she could listen to the flood of conversations that were sure to accompany the gathering.

After Theodotos offered prayer and thanksgiving, the men ate, drank, and shared among themselves.

Lydia kept cups full and removed dishes as they emptied. Between those times, she stood nearby, listening and watching.

Theodotus lay at the head of the table, relaxed and with authority in his pristine garments. Along both sides of the low table, several other priests reclined, as well as James and Peter who had been invited to share in the meal. Lydia also noticed Stephen at the far end and next to him was another of the seven; a man named Nicolaus.

Her brothers had not formally introduced her to any of the seven, besides Stephen, but she heard them speak of Nicolaus being from Antioch. He recently converted to Judaism and came to Jerusalem to celebrate Passover. While in the city, he heard of the things that happened to Jesus and recognized him as the Messiah the Jewish people had been waiting for. Though not a Jew by birth, the others could not deny the fire of Adonai's spirit that burned within Nicolaus.

Lydia drew near to refill Stephen's cup.

"Isn't it wonderful?" Stephen whispered as she bent to pour out the watered wine.

"What is?" She kept her attention on her task.

"This." Stephen waved toward the gathering.

"How so many priests have come to believe in your brother as Messiah."

Lydia glanced around the room. "They believe?"

"Yes." Stephen smiled his classic wide grin. "Theodotos has been sharing during his Temple duties, and many have received the message. They've come here tonight to hear our reports and offer funds to help in our mission to the poor in Jerusalem."

Lydia lifted the jug to herself. "That's why they're here?"

"Adonai has a wonderful way of moving in the souls of those we least expect." Stephen chuckled. "These men have been serving Him their whole lives and have now come to accept your brother as the Messiah they've been preparing for all this time."

Lydia's eyes traveled over the faces of the men with fresh sight. She'd assumed Theodotus had invited guests to simply enjoy a meal. Instead, the men gathered to celebrate their oneness in belief and aid the cause with their financial blessings, so more could be reached.

She hugged the water jug to her chest. *Oh, Adonai. Your ways are a mystery. You provide for Your own.*

CHAPTER 5

Lydia shadowed her mother, Salome, and Ria through the streets toward Naavah's home. Winter rains had lightened, and the chill did not cling to the air as long. Almond trees blossomed to reveal the transition from one season to another, though Lydia's weekly routine remained steady.

She spent the first day of the week gathered with believers in the villa listening to Peter or James share about Jesus. On the second day, she visited with Naavah, encouraging widows and displaced women who needed aid. She spent the rest of the week tending to the villa and the needs of the men so they could visit widows in the city. The last day of the week was reserved for resting and spending time with family.

With the continual financial blessing of several priests, they were able to reach more in Jerusalem and see many through the harsh winter. However, there was one face Lydia would not see in Naavah's home this week. Sherra, the older widow who rescued the Roman soldier bitten by a viper, had passed. One of the seven discovered her still lying on her mat and helped to make sure she was buried with her relatives.

Thoughts of Sherra's warm embrace and kind heart made Lydia's chest heavy. Even though Naavah's home would be filled with women, it would feel empty to her.

Naavah greeted them with kisses on their cheeks and a nice selection of fruit.

Though the dwelling was small and borrowed from her brother, once inside, Lydia's cares melted. With her meager portions, Naavah's hands were always open and her house was one of the most inviting places Lydia had ever visited in Jerusalem. Theodotus' villa paled compared to the former adulteress' home.

Women were already gathered, and Lydia recognized many faces.

"Lydia." Naavah pulled her aside. "I have a new friend I'd like to introduce you to." She escorted her across the room to where a woman stood. "This is Junia."

Drawing near, Lydia noted the woman's elaborately plaited hair and white stola peeking out from under her green palla. These revealed her as a Roman. "Greetings."

Junia dipped her head. "Naavah has shared much about you."

Lydia glanced at Naavah. "Oh?"

"She tells me you're a sister of Jesus of Nazareth," Junia continued.

"I am."

"Wonderful." She clapped her hands. "I have so many questions."

"I don't think I'm the person to answer your questions."

Junia gave Naavah a pleading glance.

Naavah leaned close to Lydia. "I told her you'd be

willing to speak with her about your brother."

"My mother is here," Lydia offered. "Surely she could answer more of your questions."

"I would like to speak with her, should she be willing." Junia's cheeks tinted pink. "But if you'd indulge me, I would like to speak with you first."

"Very well."

Naavah excused herself. "I'll leave you two to talk."

Lydia waved toward a stack of unoccupied pillows. "Shall we sit?"

Junia settled herself with the grace of royalty.

Lydia plopped down like a tired camel. "What do you want to know about Jesus?"

"Well," she clasped her hands together, "the reason I wanted to speak with you is, while I'm sure your mother could answer my questions, I know no one knows a man quite like his sister."

Lydia snickered.

"What I mean is, I want the truth and I know mothers may tend to…" she pulled her hands apart slowly, "stretch the truth."

Lydia nodded in agreement.

"My husband and I celebrated Passover in Jerusalem a few years ago, and we heard your brother teaching." Her eyes took on a glimmer. "He was so wonderful. He spoke like no rabbi we'd ever heard."

"As you know, my brother didn't sit at the feet of a rabbi."

Junia placed a gentle hand on Lydia's arm. "I understand. But there was no denying his words came from Adonai." She removed her hand. "After that, my husband and I found every opportunity to hear Jesus teach and even took part in his mission of sending seventy followers out into the cities to share his words."

Lydia recalled her brother's followers sharing the story on multiple occasions.

"Those weeks and months were some of the most exciting I've ever experienced." Her smile widened. "We were welcomed into so many homes and shared about your brother and his teachings. My husband and I even healed the sick and cast out demons." Her breath quickened. "Can you believe it? The two of us; a Hebrew and a Roman carrying Adonai's word and being used to heal."

"My brother claimed to do mighty works."

"And we got to take part in some of that work." Her gaze dropped to her lap. "Though there were many who did not welcome us or the message we carried. My heart aches for those who denied."

Lydia felt a twinge in her chest.

"Still," Junia lifted a sheepish gaze, "I want to know more. What was Jesus like before he started teaching? I want to know everything about him."

"There is not much to tell," Lydia admitted. "He was a normal boy and young man who left home one day claiming Adonai had called him to teach." Her insides ached. "To tell you the truth, his absence put a strain on our family for a long time. My brothers and sisters struggled when our mother left to follow him."

"Oh, I'm sorry." Junia reached out and squeezed Lydia's arm. "That must have hurt."

"It did." Lydia tilted her head. "It hurt even worse to see where his path led." Thoughts of her brother mixed with the new sorrow at losing Sherra. "I miss him a great deal."

"I'm sure you must." Junia gave her arm another squeeze before releasing her hold. "But we all must be obedient to Adonai."

Lydia wiped her face before she could release a single tear. "You said your husband was a Hebrew. From which tribe?"

"Benjamin," she answered with raised shoulders. "His brother relocated to Jerusalem several years ago when his son showed great promise. We often stayed with them during feasts. Though," her shoulders sagged, "after we decided to follow Jesus, they excluded us from his family."

"The same has happened to several others."

"We've continued sharing about Jesus ever since he sent us out, but when we learned of the work being done here in Jerusalem, we came back to help. Andronicus and I know well what it's like to lose family relations over following Jesus."

"Well, we could certainly use all the help Adonai is willing to send." A tingle pricked at Lydia's neck. "You said your husband is of the tribe of Benjamin?"

"Yes."

"We don't hear of many left from that tribe. Where was he born?"

"Tarsus."

Lydia's gut twisted. "Is he related to Saul ben Chislon?"

"Saul? He's our nephew."

"Nephew?" Dread clawed at her throat, drying out the word.

"His family is very proud of him." Her smile fell lopsided. "I hear he is to be appointed a seat among the Pharisees soon."

"You've heard truth." Lydia swallowed to wet her parched throat.

Junia lifted a brow. "Do you know him?"

"You could say that."

"I hope you won't hold his family's pride against us." She gave a pleading glance. "Though we share family heritage, we don't seem to share the same ideologies."

She shook her head. "As long as you don't hope my brother's divinity was hereditary."

Junia released a chuckle. "I should think not."

Lydia relaxed and eased into sharing more about Jesus. She recounted their days spent playing as children and her mother's stories surrounding his miraculous birth. She shared their struggles while he was away and the heartbreak of his death. Among Junia's questions and tales from her interactions with Jesus during his time as a rabbi, Lydia shared all that happened since her brother's resurrection.

By the time the day was spent and Lydia needed to return to the villa, she felt renewed and refreshed. Though she'd only known Junia for a single day, the two parted like old friends with embraces that neither wanted to end. The hours spent with Junia reminded Lydia of the countless ones she'd spent in Bethany with

Martha and Mary through the years. Soaking in friendship had bathed her soul in peace and restoration. Though she'd not comforted others, she knew Adonai had sent her a comforter on a day she most needed one.

Thank you, she whispered from her heart as she traveled back to the villa.

CHAPTER 6

At the peak of citrus harvest, Lydia's mother awakened her one night.

"Lydia," Mary whispered. "I need you to fetch Naomi. Elissa's time has come."

The urgency in her mother's voice clashed with the realization of her words. Lydia scrambled to her feet and quickly tied on worn sandals before rushing from the villa toward the Lower City.

Jerusalem was quiet and bathed in moonlight as Lydia scurried toward Naomi's house. She prayed the midwife would be home and not assisting someone else in the vast city.

Pounding on the wooden door, she called out, "Naomi!"

Sounds of stirring came from within.

The door creaked open and Naomi peeked her head between the crack. "Lydia?"

"It's Elissa," Lydia explained quickly. "Ima says it's her time."

"Come in." She widened the space between the door and the frame. "I'll get my supplies."

Lydia stepped into the darkened dwelling. "Anything I can do to help?"

"Grab that bag over there." She pointed to a nearby satchel. "I need to change, and then we'll fill it."

The echo of her mother's earnest words rang through her mind. "Do you think it best if we hurry?"

"First babies take their time. I'll just be a moment." Naomi ducked into a room.

Lydia snatched the bag from its place and held it open. Vapors of her dreams pulled at the edges of her mind. She'd been dreaming of a pair of ginger eyes shining from the face of a young boy. She shook away the vision as Naomi returned.

The midwife fluttered about the room, depositing various items into the bag in Lydia's hands until she was satisfied.

With hurried paces, the two women made their way back to the villa and up the stairs, where Mary cradled Elissa in her arms on the floor.

"Praise Adonai," Mary exclaimed as Naomi came into the room.

Naomi set her bag down near Elissa and went to work examining the very pregnant woman.

Lydia remained close, but out of the way.

"Let's get you up and moving," Naomi suggested.

It took all three women to assist Elissa to her feet.

"Have her walk," Naomi instructed.

Lydia slithered herself under Elissa's arm to support her sister-in-law. "Easy."

Elissa's breath came in short bursts as she shuffled around the room with one arm wrapped around Lydia's shoulders and the other cradling her midsection. "The pains are growing intense."

"I think that's supposed to happen," Lydia offered. She eyed Naomi and Mary whispering to each other.

Though neither woman's face revealed true dread, their expressions were uneasy as they spoke in hushed tones.

Lydia thought it best to keep Elissa preoccupied. "How long have you felt the pain?"

"Several hours," Elissa answered and then moaned. She halted and rubbed her stomach. "That was a big one."

"Come on," Lydia encouraged. "Naomi said you need to walk." She kept her back straight as she helped bear Elissa's weight. "Have you thought of names?"

"James and I have spoken of a few." She scrunched at another wave of pain. "Did you send word to my father?"

In her hurry to fetch Naomi, Lydia forgot to rouse Benjamin from his slumber in the next house over from the midwife. "Naomi mentioned this could take a while. We could send word to him after."

"Please?" Elissa pleaded with the intensity of a begging child. "It would mean the world to place my child upon his lap."

"Of course," Lydia conceded. She eased Elissa's arm over her head. "I'll fetch him." Leaving her sister-in-law's side, she interrupted Naomi and her mother. "I'm going to fetch Benjamin." Lydia tossed a glance over her shoulder. "Elissa's request."

"Hurry back," Mary's words bordered on demanding. "We might need your assistance."

Lydia let her head dip to one side. "What help could I be?"

Mary glanced at Naomi.

"I'm a little concerned," Naomi admitted in a whisper. "I might need all the extra hands I can get with this delivery."

Lydia looked at Elissa, who was clutching the stone wall for support. "I'll be back as quickly as I can."

True to her word, Lydia rushed from the villa and ran toward Benjamin's house.

Her rapid pounding on his door stirred the old potter. "Who has disturbed my slumber?"

"Benjamin, come quickly," Lydia protested. "It's Elissa. She sends for you."

"The baby?" Benjamin stepped out into the open air. "Is Elissa well?"

"Her time has come," Lydia explained. "She has not delivered yet, but she sent me to fetch you. Naomi is with her already. We need to hurry."

With no need for further prodding, Lydia led Benjamin through the twisting streets toward the priest's villa.

Upon entering, Lydia saw many of the household gathered in the main area. Some were bowed in prayer, while others talked amongst themselves. She made her way to Salome. "What's happened?"

Elissa's groans carried down the stairs.

"We were all awakened by Elissa's cries." Salome wiped at her drooping eyes.

"The baby is coming," Lydia clarified for her younger sister. "Naomi's with her, and I fetched her father." She inclined her head toward Benjamin, who was speaking with James. "We'd better get upstairs."

"We?" Salome's eyes popped open.

"Naomi wants helping hands." She lifted her palms. "It's not like you'll be able to go back to sleep anyway."

Salome looked toward the upper room as Elissa released another loud wail into the night. "I suppose you're right."

The two ascended the stairs together.

Lydia entered the room and found Elissa squatting. She made her way toward her. "Your father is downstairs." She wiped away damp hair from her sister-in-law's face. "I've brought Salome to help."

Salome nestled next to Elissa and grabbed her hand. "Soon we shall meet the newest member of the family."

Lydia walked toward Naomi. "Any update?"

"We're in for a long night." The midwife dug through her bag.

"Many are downstairs praying."

Naomi nodded with a sigh of relief. "I'll take Adonai's help tonight as well."

Lydia lifted a silent plea of mercy on Elissa's behalf and the strength to provide comfort for the ailing mother-to-be.

Through the next several hours, Lydia took turns with the other women supporting Elissa and assisting Naomi. When Enoch the rooster crowed with the rising sun, Naomi set a baby boy on Elissa's chest.

Lydia took in the sight of the newborn wiggling upon his mother. He had dark hair and an olive complexion like the rest of the family.

Tears streamed down Elissa's flushed face. "Praise

You, Adonai."

Naomi wiped her forehead with the back of her stained hand. "Praise Him for strength, Elissa. I was worried you weren't going to be able to deliver this one alone."

Mary watched the boy suckle. "I suppose he was enjoying all the citrus Elissa's been eating." She giggled. "Perhaps he wanted to taste some for himself."

After being allowed to enjoy his first meal, Naomi cleaned and wrapped the infant with Mary's help.

"Can I hold him?" Salome whispered.

Elissa smiled. "Of course."

Naomi gently set the bundle in her young arms. "Mind his head."

Salome pulled the little one close to herself and sat cross-legged beside Elissa. "He's so perfect."

Elissa simply nodded.

Lydia gazed over the wrappings. "That was amazing, Elissa. You're so strong."

Elissa's eyes grew heavy. "You'll be able to do it one day, too."

A twinge pricked at Lydia's inside. She wasn't so sure she could do what Elissa had accomplished. Even in the experienced midwife's estimation, the young woman shouldn't have been able to safely bring forth the boy. He'd grown quite large inside his mother's womb. Lydia wasn't even sure she wanted children of her own. Though a pair of shining ginger eyes danced in her vision.

"Let your sister have a turn," Mary instructed.

Salome lifted the baby toward Lydia.

"Me?" Lydia put a hand on her chest and looked at Elissa.

The new mother softly snored against the stack of pillows Naomi had placed behind her.

"Go ahead," Mary encouraged.

Lydia held out trembling hands and accepted the baby into her arms. She tucked him in close to her chest. Gazing down, she stared into the face of her nephew.

He adjusted to the movement, but settled down with a small yawn.

His round, little mouth was the cutest thing Lydia had ever seen. "He looks a lot like James," she admitted with a smile.

Mary leaned over. "He sure does."

"Benjamin and James are waiting downstairs," Salome reminded the group of women.

An ache grew in Lydia's arms. She'd only just received the precious bundle, and she already had to let him go. Her hold tightened around the boy as she leaned in to place a kiss on his soft cheek. Reluctantly, she released him into Mary's extended arms.

Mary nuzzled the baby. "I only wish Joseph were here to meet him." She led the women downstairs to the others.

Lydia took her place among the gathering as Mary presented the young one to Benjamin, who was seated in waiting.

The old potter laid the boy in his lap and covered his head with his hands as he spoke a blessing over the firstborn.

Lydia recalled seeing her father bless Simon and Salome in much the same way when they joined the family. Her heart ached at the memory of his face. His deep voice echoed through her mind, bringing bittersweet sorrow to the celebration.

Eight days later, they gathered with other Way Followers around the parents. After Rabbi Ethan performed the circumcision and returned the crying boy to his mother for comfort, he spoke a blessing over the family.

Elissa shifted her son into her husband's arms for the final tradition.

James cradled the growing boy and, with a wide smile, declared his name, "He shall be called Joshua ben James." He looked into the face of his son. "Named for a great leader of our people, and so we pray Adonai will use him as such."

Lydia smiled. She'd always wondered how parents selected the names of their children. Many repeated names from generation to generation, while others started new traditions. In a wonderful way, the name seemed to fit the boy perfectly.

Joshua, she whispered to Adonai. *May he walk in Your ways all the days of his life.*

CHAPTER 7

Several weeks later, Lydia hurried through the villa toward the outer court to check on Michal. She stopped milking the female goat two months prior to give the animal rest before her delivery. Michal had been showing signs that the end of her pregnancy was nearing. Lydia knew she would soon bring forth a new life.

She scurried through the courtyard and finally found Michal lying under the covering. "There you are." She slowed her approach. "Do you have something to show me?"

"Baa," Michal answered with a swing of her head.

Curled up next to her was a pile of brown fur.

"Oh." Lydia moved closer. "I see we have a new arrival at the villa."

Hearing her voice, the small bundle lifted his head and looked at her.

"Shalom, little one." Lydia squatted to get a better look but kept a respectful distance.

Another head emerged from behind Michal. This one was white with brown spots.

"Oh, my." Lydia put a hand on her chest. "Twins."

Michal lifted herself from the hay and waddled toward Lydia with a full udder.

Seeing their meal leave, the two young kids

stumbled to their legs and gave chase.

Lydia chuckled as she watched the newborn goats practice walking on shaky hooves. "Would you look at them?" Settling down, she carefully inspected the kids. "Well done, Michal. Your boys look very healthy and strong."

Michal brought them closer.

Daring a light touch, Lydia stroked both goats. Their fur was the softest she had felt in a long time. "And what shall we call you?" She set a finger on her lips. "You know, there's a story about Jacob breeding spotted sheep… and goats," she quickly added. "He was a twin, too." She looked at the white one. "I'll call you Jacob and," she glanced toward the larger brown one, "you will be Esau."

"Baa," he cried.

"Don't worry. I know you will bring redemption to the name." She indulged in another pat to both kids and a good scratch behind Michal's ear. "Sorry, I can't stay long. We're going to the Temple today." She rose to her feet and dusted off her backside. "My nephew is being dedicated to Adonai." Her smile widened. "My nephew," she repeated. "I'm an aunt."

She made her way back inside and exchanged her tunic for a clean one her mother had prepared the previous day. It wasn't new, but the old garment looked better after a good scrub.

Borrowing Salome's comb, she detangled her hair and fashioned a simple braid. She dabbed some balsam oil on her neck before adding a head covering. Checking her reflection in her small bronze mirror, she gave a simple nod of approval and followed her family to the Temple.

The large, white building sparkled in the rays of the Adar morning. People flowed in and out of the gates at all points throughout the day. There was always a sacrifice or prayer to be given at the feet of Adonai.

A low rumble in her stomach reminded Lydia of the day. The dedication of Joshua fell on the Fast of Esther. This day was one of remembrance of the bravery of Queen Esther and the victory of the Jews against the schemes of Haman to end their race. Though tradition held this day as a minor fast day, many in Jerusalem submitted to the one-day fast before enjoying the merriment that would follow for the next two days.

Lydia counted herself among those who abstained from food until the setting sun. She knew her family was planning a feast for the evening meal to celebrate Joshua's dedication.

James led the group up the stairs and through the Court of Gentiles.

Lydia could feel pride rolling off him like waves. She'd never seen her older brother smile more or hold his head as high. His son was only forty days old, but James looked at him as if he were the greatest treasure in the world.

Jude followed the proud father, discussing where they would visit after the ceremony and leading a young lamb behind him.

Lydia's thoughts turned to Jesus. She wondered if

her brother was happy with the news of a nephew among them. The ache in her heart pressed forward. She missed talking to Jesus. He never dismissed her, as the others had a habit of doing.

As they neared the Beautiful Gate, her attention drifted to Arava. The mute, deaf betrothed of Jude followed the group and seemed content to simply exist among them. She was a hard worker and never complained. Though Lydia wondered how the woman would express her protests if she had them. Salome and Jude seemed to be the only ones who understood her hand gestures.

Salome signaled to Arava as they walked.

Lydia was curious about the private language, but not enough to invade their privacy. The two women gave the impression of being in a world of their own. One in which Lydia did not always feel welcomed.

Climbing the enormous steps, Lydia's thoughts turned to Assia. Her oldest sister had been escorted back to Nazareth and into the arms of her husband. As Passover approached, she wondered if the couple would travel to Jerusalem for the upcoming feasts. She was sure Joseph extended the invitation as he traveled around Galilee, spreading the call to the disciples' families. She wasn't sure if Assia would be so eager to return.

They paused in the Court of Women.

Elissa made her way toward the colonnades surrounding the court. There she located the Trumpet Chest designated for bird offerings and deposited a coin into the wide mouth opening.

The familiar rattle of metal on metal sounded as the coin circled the trumpet and dropped into the wooden chest. Somewhere on the other side of the Nicanor Gate that separated the Court of Women from the Priest's Courtyard, a dove would be sacrificed as a sin offering to restore Elissa's ceremonial condition.

Jude tugged at the rope attached to the lamb they'd purchased for the dedication sacrifice.

As he directed the animal past Lydia, she realized the innocent creature did not know what fate awaited him. He quietly followed them through the streets of Jerusalem and into the Temple without a care. In a few brief moments, his time among them would end. He would be offered as a burnt offering on the altar of Adonai.

Her heart squeezed, peering down into the animal's large, dark eyes. She had no way of communicating to him her displeasure for such requirements, though expressing her feelings would not change the situation. She looked at her nephew cradled in his father's arms and then back at the young lamb.

Blood to cover blood. Something whispered in her soul.

A shiver raced down her back. She knew of the countless sacrifices that had been made in this Temple and of all the ones her ancestors made in the Tabernacle. Though Adonai required blood as payment for restoration, she knew of far too many Gentile gods who required the blood of children instead of animals. Looking at the helpless face of her nephew, she was grateful for that mercy.

As the men entered the Gate, Lydia noticed James remove a money pouch from his tunic. Though she'd never seen the ritual that took place inside the Priest's Courtyard, she'd heard enough accounts to know what happened beyond the elaborately decorated doors.

The pouch contained five precious shekels that would be used as payment to redeem Joshua.

She knew Adonai told Moses, "Consecrate to me all the firstborn. Whatever is the first to open the womb among the people of Israel, both of man and of beast, is mine."

James would present his son to the priest, who then exchanged the child for the coins. In this, the firstborn would be released from their obligation to be given to Adonai. They would, instead, be returned to their father's arms.

Lydia's attention drifted to her mother.

Mary stood chatting with the other women as they waited for the men to return.

From the stories of her childhood, Lydia knew her mother had purchased two doves the day they brought Jesus to the Temple for this same ceremony. They were poor and could barely afford the cost. Mary also shared of Simeon and Anna, two who had waited for years to bless Jesus as the One for whom their people had been waiting.

She glanced at the gate overlaid with Corinthian bronze and imagined the scene unfolding on the other side as Joshua was redeemed.

Images of a money pouch struck her. Jesus had been redeemed with five shekels as a child, but he was later purchased for thirty pieces.

Blood to cover blood. The internal voice whispered again.

Gazing once more at her mother, she wondered if Mary knew that day, with Simeon and Anna's voices ringing in her ears, that her Lamb would give His blood to cover so many others.

CHAPTER 8

Lydia's weeks were filled with preparations for the families coming from Galilee. Among her daily chores and weekly visits with Naavah, she helped prepare rooms in the villa and store food and supplies that sprung forth from the change of season and the continued generosity of the priests.

Joseph returned to Jerusalem only days before Passover with several members of the disciples' families.

As people poured into the villa, Lydia caught sight of one woman waddling through the doors, very much in her last days of pregnancy.

"Assia!" She burst through the crowd and wrapped her sister in a tight embrace. Before the birth of Joshua, she would have kept her distance, but her nephew had dug out a new place in her heart and soul.

"Miss me?" Assia chuckled in her ear. "I've not been gone that long."

Lydia held her out at arm's length. "Look at you."

Assia wrapped her arms around her stomach. "Can you believe it?"

"Of course I can," Lydia teased. "Being a mother is all you've talked about since I can remember." She placed a hand on her sister's round stomach. "What I can't believe is that you would travel such a distance, being so near your time."

Assia's attention flicked to their mother, who was smothering Joseph in affectionate kisses. "Ima came all this way to give birth to Jesus in Bethlehem." She let her eyes wander back to Lydia. "I wanted to give birth among my family."

"Ima was forced to travel here by Caesar Augustus and his tax census," she reminded her sister. "You could have stayed tucked away among your new family."

"It's not the same." Assia squeezed Lydia's hand and gazed around the open area. "I wanted my child to experience this."

Lydia followed her gaze. She watched as greetings and introductions were exchanged in a chaos of embraces and kisses. Husbands were reunited with wives and children, and families were made whole once more. What choice would she have made had she stood in her sister's place?

"Come," Assia's voice broke through Lydia's thoughts. "I'll introduce you to some of the others."

Lydia submitted to her sister's leading.

First, she was presented to Peter's family. His wife, Hannah, was a round-faced woman with bright eyes and a loud laugh. She came with her mother, Miriam, and they were quick to share how Jesus healed her years ago.

Hiding in the folds of Hannah's dress was their young daughter.

Bending low, Lydia bowed. "Shalom, little one. What's your name?"

"Petronilla," she squeaked.

Lydia looked up at Hannah. "How many harvests has she seen?"

"Four." Hannah reached down and brushed at her daughter's hair. "She was born just before Peter began to follow Jesus."

Lydia whispered to Petronilla, "Do you like animals?"

The girl's dark hair bounced with a nod.

"Remind me to introduce you to some of my friends later." She winked.

Petronilla smiled widely.

Lydia was introduced to Andrew's wife Ruth and Philip's wife Shoshana. Both seemed lovely enough and were excited to take up residence in Jerusalem.

When the noise of reunification settled, Joseph reported well wishes and apologized on behalf of those who had elected to remain in Galilee. Some sent along word that they would visit Jerusalem at another time, while others offered funds in place of their presence. James and John's father Zebedee was one of those who provided a large financial gift.

Joseph handed a large money pouch to James.

Pulling the bag to his chest, he prayed aloud, "May these gifts bring glory to Adonai."

Lydia turned to Assia. "There is one family member you haven't met yet."

"Oh?" Assia's eyes took on a shine.

Grabbing her hand, she pulled her sister deeper into the house.

Settled at a low table, Elissa was feeding Joshua.

"Assia," Lydia waved to Elissa, "may I present Joshua ben James?"

"Truly?" Assia moved closer to Elissa. "You've had a son?"

Elissa nodded as she unlatched Joshua from her chest and held him up.

The small boy wiggled in his mother's arms.

Assia held out her hands. "May I?"

"Of course." Elissa surrendered the boy to her.

Looking into the face of her nephew, Assia wept.

"Why are you crying?" Lydia asked.

Assia wiped at her face. "I'm just so happy." She pulled Joshua to her chest and nestled her nose into his neck.

Lydia shook her head. "You've got a funny way of showing it."

A laugh erupted from Assia. "One day, when you're full of life, you'll understand."

A set of ginger eyes flashed in Lydia's mind. "Perhaps."

"He's beautiful." Assia held the boy up for inspection. "And he looks a lot like James."

Joshua whimpered.

"And he's got his father's appetite." Elissa reached for her son and returned him to her chest.

With much care, Assia settled next to Elissa. "Is Ima pleased?"

Lydia moved a pillow to the other side of Elissa and sat upon it. "She hovers over the two of them like a mother hen." She flicked her attention to the assembly, still chattering in the next room. "The arrival of the others has been poor Elissa's first reprieve from her attention since he was born."

"Your mother's not that bad," Elissa defended. "She simply cares a great deal."

"Mark my words," Lydia offered. "She'll be worse once your child arrives, sister."

"I can't wait." Assia cradled her stomach. "So, what other news is there?"

Lydia considered all that happened in her sister's absence. "Jude has taken a betrothed."

Assia's eyebrows jumped. "Truly?"

"Arava."

"I had my suspicions that she was taken with Jude." She rubbed her belly. "But how did James get her family to agree to the match?"

"He didn't," Lydia admitted. "The situation is…" she searched for the right word, "…unique."

"Speak on."

"Her family cast her out when they discovered Jude had brought her to Peter for healing. They considered her a Way Follower." She looked across the room at the quiet young girl. "Jude found her living on the streets and brought her here." Her gaze returned to her sister. "She's a hard worker, and I'm sure she'll make a fine wife for Jude." She let her gaze slowly drop. "I still wonder sometimes why it didn't work."

"Why what didn't work?"

"The healing." Lydia let her attention go back to Arava. "The men have healed so many others. Why not her?"

Assia drew shapes on her round stomach. "It is not

for us to know the mind of Adonai. There will always be mysteries known only to Him."

"Still," Lydia sighed, "they are to be married soon. Jude wanted to wait until after Passover. He was hoping many of the families would come to join the work being done in Jerusalem. At least, once they are married, she will have a permanent place in a family again."

"And a wonderful family at that," Elissa added. "I know I couldn't have asked for better."

"Tell me more," Assia begged.

Elissa removed the satisfied boy from her chest and set him on her shoulder. "A few months ago, the men set apart seven to help them with the Hellenistic widows."

"Have there been more in need?" Concerned dripped from Assia's question.

"Many," Lydia answered. "It was a harsh season, and we are aware of several who were being overlooked. Though the newly selected men have helped to lighten the load by visiting widows so the others can teach and share in the city."

"I'm sure you'll have a chance to meet the seven soon," Elissa added. "One of them has taken notice of your sister." She fluttered her lashes at Lydia.

"Elissa!" Lydia shrieked.

"Sister," Assia squealed. "Is this true?"

"No!" Lydia protested and folded her arms across her chest. "It's absolutely not true."

Assia turned to Elissa. "Is it true?"

"It most certainly is."

Lydia felt heat rise on the sides of her neck. "Stop jesting."

"I don't jest." Elissa put a hand to her chest. "I've seen the way the man looks at you."

"Oh, sister," Assia urged. "Tell me about him."

Lydia stuck her nose in the air, refusing to indulge her sister's curiosity.

"I don't know much about him," Elissa answered on her behalf. "But from what I've seen, he is a man filled with Adonai's spirit and faith in Jesus. He's kind and compassionate. The others speak of his care when attending the widows."

"He sounds quite wonderful," Assia admitted.

Lowering her face, Lydia folded into herself. "That's why he can't possibly be interested in me."

Assia leaned over Elissa. "Why do you say such an untrue thing?"

"Because it is true." Lydia lifted watery eyes. "No man that good would ever want me as his wife."

"Well, that's simply not true," Assia argued. "Any man would be lucky to take you as his bride."

"Truly?" Lydia wiped away the unbidden tears.

"I know we haven't always seen the world the same," Assia reached for her sister, "but I count you dear to my heart and would love to see you find happiness in this life."

Lydia held her sister's arm across Elissa, wrapping the two in an embrace. For much of her life, she'd felt out of place and dismissed. At that moment, her heart opened to the possibility that Adonai might have a plan for her, just as He revealed His plans for her siblings.

CHAPTER 9

With Passover complete, and the newest residents of the villa settled and eager to help with daily tasks, Lydia received approval from James to visit Bethany. Her older brother agreed to let her be the one to invite Lazarus and his sisters to Jude's wedding feast with a stipulation; Stephen would escort her. With the influx of visitors to the city for the feast days, the brothers were too busy to make the trip to Bethany themselves.

She reluctantly agreed to the terms; grateful for the freedom and the company, even if she was unsure of how Stephen felt about the arrangement.

The journey through the streets of Jerusalem and out of the Golden Gate was quiet. It wasn't until the two entered the Kidron Valley that either of them spoke.

Stephen was the one to break the silence. "Have you known Lazarus and his family for a long time?"

"Oh, yes." Lydia beamed. "Martha is my very dearest friend."

"I was there the day your brother raised Lazarus from the dead."

She turned eager eyes on him. "You were?"

"It was one of the most incredible things I've ever seen. To watch someone wrapped in grave clothes just walk right out of a tomb." He shook his head. "I mean, if anyone there had any doubts about your brother before that moment, I'm sure they didn't afterward."

"I wouldn't know." She lifted a shoulder. "I wasn't there."

"James talks a lot about that regret," he openly admitted. "But it's understandable."

Lydia lifted a brow.

"I mean, we've been looking for a King, not a craftsman." He stepped carefully over a rough part of the path and hesitated as he waited for Lydia to clear it, too. "Even though your family spent many years with Jesus, I'm sure He wasn't the type to boast about His position."

A flood of memories washed over Lydia, tiny moments that pointed to her brother's difference among them. She had missed them all, but she wasn't the only one. "I miss Him," she confessed.

"Of course you do." Stephen half turned toward her as they walked. "Jesus was your brother." He returned his attention to the path.

"Tell me about your family."

Stephen slowed his pace.

"If you don't mind," Lydia hurried to add.

"I suppose they're as plain as any family." He picked up his previous stride. "My father's family came from Cyrene to Jerusalem. He owns an inn in the northern part of the city. Most of my family helps him run it. I already shared that I have five older brothers. They're all married with children, which makes for many helping hands."

"I'm sure it does."

"Let's see. What else can I share?" He folded his arms across his chest. "My family attends the synagogue of the Freedmen."

"I'm not familiar with that synagogue."

"They're from all over; Cyrene, Alexandria, Cilicia. Most are descendants of Jews who were freed from their Roman masters and returned to Jerusalem."

"We often visit Rabbi Ethan's synagogue."

Stephen nodded. "Jude speaks highly of his rabbi."

"I think most rabbis are the same."

Stephen chuckled. "We have many wonderful speakers at our synagogue." He rubbed the back of his neck. "W-would you be interested in visiting sometime?"

She tilted her head. "Visit your synagogue?"

"Yes." He stopped. "I'd love for you to attend and maybe even meet my family." His ginger eyes shone as bright as his smile.

Lydia's insides fluttered. She wasn't sure if that meant she truly had feelings for this man or if she'd unknowingly swallowed some poor creature on their trek through the valley. "S-sure," she stammered.

"Wonderful."

During the rest of the journey, Lydia and Stephen swapped stories about their families and childhoods.

Before she knew it, Bethany came into view. Lydia took the lead, directing their steps to Lazarus' home.

"Greetings to the owner of this house," she called on their approach.

"Lydia!" Martha yelled, running toward them from the side of the house.

Lydia wrapped her friend in a tight embrace and received multiple kisses on her cheeks. No matter how unwelcomed she felt sometimes in the villa, a trip to Bethany always felt like a second home.

"Shame on you." Martha wagged her finger at Lydia and set a disapproving frown on her face. "Your family moved to Jerusalem, and I've seen you now as much as when you lived all the way in Nazareth."

A twinge of guilt vibrated through Lydia. "James keeps us all busy."

"And how is our dear friend? Hmm?" Her temporary scorn melted into pleasantness. "Still attempting to lift the burden of everyone in Jerusalem?"

"With the help of Joseph, Jude, and all Jesus' followers."

Stephen cleared his throat.

"Oh." Lydia turned toward the sound. In her rapture catching up with Martha, she'd almost forgotten her traveling companion. "Martha, I'd like to introduce you to Stephen."

"Shalom." Martha dipped her head.

"I've heard so much about your family," Stephen confessed.

"Only the good, I hope." Martha nudged Lydia with her elbow.

Lydia brushed off her friend's jest. "Stephen is one of the seven men James and Peter selected to help tend to the widows," she explained. "They were spread thin attempting to teach and aid the less fortunate."

"Well," Martha flashed a bright smile, "any friend

of Lydia's is welcome here." She waved toward her home. "Come, come."

Martha led the two inside and set out food and drink before settling among them.

"Is your brother here?" Stephen asked, reaching for a piece of goat's milk cheese.

"Ever since Jesus healed Lazarus, my brother has hardly stayed in one place long." Martha helped herself to a slice of citron. "He spends much of his days out in the fields."

Lydia looked around. "And your sister?"

"Mary went to the market." Martha took a sip from her cup. "She'll be sad she missed your visit."

"Well," Lydia reached for a handful of almonds, "the main reason I came today was to invite your family to Jude's wedding feast."

Martha choked on her drink. "Wedding Feast?"

"You didn't know he was betrothed?" Lydia tilted her head.

Martha set her hands on her broad hips. "If you don't visit your poor friend in Bethany with such news, how's she to know?"

"Forgive me." Lydia's cheeks warmed. "I thought James and Lazarus had been speaking."

"Lazarus sees less of his friends than I do mine." She squinted her eyes.

"Then you shall have to convince your brother to leave his fields for a few days and come join the celebration."

"It seems your family has had many celebrations lately." Martha lifted her cup to her mouth once more and her eyebrows followed the upward movement.

Lydia thought for a moment. "We've had feasts for James and Elissa. Joseph got to attend Assia's feast in Nazareth. Now it's Jude's turn to join with Arava." More celebrations came to her. "James and Elissa welcomed a little boy only weeks ago."

"Praise Adonai." Martha clapped. "What did they call him?"

"Joshua."

"Oh," Martha squealed. "Little Joshua ben James."

"Everyone says he looks just like his father. You'll get to meet him at the feast." Lydia's eyes widened. "Assia has also come for a visit and she is very much with child."

"I will be praying for her." Martha got quiet for a moment. "And what about our Joseph?"

"Joseph has always been one to take his time," Lydia admitted. "I'm not sure if he's ready to take a wife just yet."

Martha hummed.

"Though I've seen him with a friend of ours, and he seems quite taken with her."

"Oh?"

Lydia nodded. "But it's a bit of a complicated situation."

"How complicated could it be?"

"Do you remember the woman Jesus rescued from stoning?"

"Of course."

Lydia raised one eyebrow.

"Joseph's taken with the adulteress?"

"I said it was complicated."

"I should say so." Martha gave a quick nod. "Poor Joseph."

"Oh, don't get me wrong," Lydia added. "Naavah is a wonderful woman. She opens her home to those who are not welcomed at the Temple, and she has such an open hand toward the poor." She ran her fingers across the edge of her cup. "Still, it's not a simple life for her."

The room was silent for several moments.

Lydia looked up into the waiting gaze of Martha.

"And what about you?" Martha slid a glance to Stephen. "Any wedding feasts in your future?"

On reflex, Lydia looked at Stephen.

He was content to enjoy Martha's offerings without adding to the conversation.

Lydia quickly returned her attention to her friend. "Nothing official."

Martha's smile widened, and she nodded in quiet approval.

For the next hour, Lydia did her best to share with Martha all that happened since their last time together. She left with the promise of more frequent visits and joy at Martha's promise that her family would attend Jude's wedding feast.

Departing Bethany, Lydia apologized to Stephen. "I'm sorry you had to endure women babbling about wedding feasts and such."

"No apology needed." He lifted his chin. "I enjoyed meeting your friend. Though it's a shame I didn't get the chance to meet Lazarus."

"Remind me during the feast, and I will introduce you."

Stephen paused. "I'm invited?"

"Of course." Lydia halted and turned toward him. "James always invites the followers to our feasts."

"The others, sure." Stephen began at a slower pace. "But me?"

"You're part of the group, too."

Stephen lifted a shoulder. "It's still odd thinking of myself as part of such an incredible collection of men."

The familiar feeling of being on the outside of a group washed through Lydia.

"Thank you for the privilege of escorting you." Stephen picked up his stride. "I enjoyed myself. Martha has a gift for hospitality."

Lydia smiled despite herself. "She truly does."

CHAPTER 10

In a few days, the villa was transformed into a colorful space fit for a wedding feast. The many hands of the disciples' families made light work of the long lists of tasks. With the burden at the villa lifted, the men spent more time in the streets of Jerusalem teaching and sharing about Jesus. The separated seven put the recent funds to work right away, buying food, clothing, and supplies for repairs for the widows.

Lydia arranged flowers in the open area of the villa, adjusting the final touches before the room would be filled with family and friends. Thinking of the faces of all those who planned to be in attendance warmed her from the inside, but there was a small place that tugged at her. Simon and Jesus were the missing pieces that prevented the week from being the ultimate celebration. Though she knew exactly where Jesus was, the location of Simon was still a mystery.

Joseph claimed the dagger wound to his midsection last year was from their wayward brother, but no one had seen Simon since. Her older brother had healed physically of his injury, but Lydia couldn't help but think Joseph had not completely healed from his encounter with Simon.

For every widow brought back from the edge of starvation, she wondered if Simon was eating enough.

For every roof patched, she wondered where Simon laid his head. For every report of another person hearing about Jesus, she wondered where Simon's loyalties lie. Her younger brother's needs had been her responsibility for years. With him gone, she felt a strange emptiness.

"Those are lovely," Stephen's voice came from behind her.

Lydia turned over her shoulder and saw him pointing at the red anemones in her hand. "They are." She adjusted the last ones into place. "All this rain has been good for them."

"I hope you don't mind that I arrived early." His cheeks bloomed against his olive complexion. "I didn't want to miss my chance at meeting Lazarus."

She smiled, taking him in. He wore a clean tunic and his hair and beard were freshly oiled. The distinct scent of cypress drifted off him, but not in an overpowering way. "The rest of our guests should arrive soon."

Stephen's eyes trailed around the room. "You've done a great job."

"We've had a lot of help lately."

"How's everyone settling in?"

Lydia nodded as she gazed around the room. "A little cramped, but we're making it work. The new arrivals have been so helpful."

His gaze came back to her slowly. "Have you thought about my offer?"

Lydia's heart sped up. "Offer?"

"To visit the synagogue."

"Oh." She let out her breath. "Yes, I have." She picked at a stray anemone's petal. "If one of my brothers escorts me, I should be able to visit."

"Soon?"

She smiled, twirling the petal between her fingers. "Soon."

"I look forward to it. Well," he lifted a shoulder, "I suppose I should let you finish your preparations."

"I'll find you when Lazarus arrives."

"Until then." He inclined his head toward her before departing.

As the sun dipped into the horizon, guests filled the villa. Laughter and music mixed with the vows of Jude and Arava.

Rabbi Ethan spent weeks practicing gestures from Salome and Jude to communicate with Arava during the ceremony.

Lydia watched light fill the young woman's eyes when the rabbi slowly motioned to her as he spoke.

Cheers bounced around the space as the couple exchanged promises to one another through hand motions.

Lydia chided herself for not taking the time to learn some of the girl's signs before the feast. After tonight, Arava would be her newest sister-in-law and she could barely talk to her. How was she to welcome her into the family with no way to communicate? She decided it was time to ask Salome for a few lessons.

With the wedding ritual complete, the guests were invited to enjoy the feast.

Lydia searched the crowd for Stephen. She found

him sampling the delicacies laid out on the low tables. "Ready to meet Lazarus?" She waved to her family friends who were laughing with Jude on the other side of the room.

He hurriedly shoved an olive into his mouth and nodded.

Making her way through the crowd with Stephen at her back, Lydia brought him to meet Lazarus.

Martha was the first to notice their approach and welcomed them with a warm smile and a gentle indication for the others to direct their attention to Lydia.

With a grateful nod in her friend's direction, Lydia made the long-awaited introduction. "Lazarus, this is Stephen; one of the seven."

"Ahhh," Lazarus released a long acknowledgement and bowed toward Stephen. "Jude was just sharing about the calling of you seven." He chuckled. "It seems Peter was unhappy serving tables."

Stephen let out an awkward laugh. "A gifted speaker like Peter should spend his time teaching."

"That may be true," Lazarus agreed. "But serving keeps a man humble."

"I couldn't agree more."

Lydia smiled. She prayed for the two men to get along, and they seemed to enjoy one another.

"You know," Stephen added, "I was there the day Jesus called you back to life."

Lydia watched a wave of something wash over Lazarus' face.

"A miracle in more than one way," Lazarus

explained. "My Lord gave me back my life and restored my body. I've never been the same, and I'm so grateful."

Martha dabbed at her eyes.

"Weep not, sister." Lazarus put his arm around Martha's shoulders. "Jesus gave us back to each other, and we should spend every day blessing Adonai for the gift."

"I know." Martha wiped again at her face. "I don't think I will ever forget the sight of you walking out of that tomb."

"Nor will I," Mary agreed.

Lydia felt an unexpected twinge in her chest. Her brother also walked out of a tomb, but she hadn't been there to see it. The last time she saw Jesus, He was lifted into the clouds with the promise of return hanging on His lips. With each passing day, her doubt overtook her faith in His words.

"We should be celebrating," Mary reminded them. "This is Jude's wedding feast." She inclined her cup toward Jude.

The bride-groom looked around. "I suppose I should find Arava before this crowd swallows her."

Lydia took the opportunity to excuse herself as well, giving Stephen the chance to get more acquainted with Lazarus and his two sisters.

The first night of feasting led into a second, though the sizable crowd had dwindled slightly.

Stephen returned, seeking an audience with Lazarus and swapping stories of Jesus and His followers.

Lydia stole away as many moments as she could with them between helping the others serve.

As the evening drew late, Lydia noticed Assia panting heavily. "Are you well, sister?" She brushed away damp hair from Assia's forehead.

"I'm no midwife." She rubbed at her large stomach. "But I'd say my time draws near."

"I'll inform Ima." Lydia hurried through the villa and relayed the news to her mother.

Mary began preparations for the new arrival and instructed the others on how they could help.

With Naomi already in attendance for the feast, Lydia didn't have to race through the streets to fetch her. She helped escort her sister to the upper room, where she could give birth apart from Jude's celebration.

Among a room full of women, Assia delivered a healthy baby.

Naomi lifted the tiny bundle onto her mother's chest. "A girl!"

Assia clasped her arms around her daughter.

"She couldn't have waited a few more nights?" Salome asked above the praise. "It's still Jude and Arava's feast."

"Perhaps she heard all the merriment and wanted to join the celebration," Lydia answered.

Naomi cleaned and wrapped the girl in fresh linens and gave her into Mary's arms.

"Welcome, little one," Mary cooed over her second grandchild. "We are so blessed you've decided to be part of the family."

When it was Lydia's turn, she gazed into the dark eyes of her niece. She was a perfect blend of Assia and Hiskiel. "She's beautiful, sister." Lydia allowed fresh tears to wash her face. "Truly she is."

After being passed from one set of open arms to the next, the girl made her way back into her mother's arms for her first meal.

Lydia floated down the stairs in rapture and awe at the process of giving life. She'd seen it more in the past few months than she had in a long time. Witnessing all these births and marriages, mixed with the beauty of Jesus' followers continuing to grow, warmed her insides with peace. Truly Adonai was blessing her family.

CHAPTER 11

At the end of the marriage feast week, Jude and Arava agreed to accompany Lydia to the synagogue of the Freedmen. They had been excused from their daily tasks to enjoy their marriage week, and James believed them to be the least needed for one more day.

Stephen met them at the villa to escort them to the synagogue. "I'm so glad you'll be attending today. I've heard there is a special speaker."

"I'm looking forward to it." Jude gestured to Arava.

Lydia understood a few of the signs now, but she was still learning and couldn't quite make out what her brother was communicating to his new wife. Salome had taught her a few of the simpler ones, but some signs made no sense to her. It was as if they had created their own language.

"Shall we?" Stephen waved toward the street.

Lydia took up the place beside him, wanting to give space for Jude to walk next to Arava.

"James tells me Assia had a daughter," Stephen shared.

"She did." Lydia was a little taken aback at how easily Stephen fell into a conversation with her as if they'd been friends their entire lives.

"What did they call her?"

She thought about the chosen name that rang

through the villa that morning. "Hadassah."

"The Hebrew name of our dear Queen Esther. A name worthy of a princess." He set a brisk pace. "It seems your family enjoys such types of names."

She considered the names of her other family members. "Oh, you mean Salome? Named after Queen Salome Alexandra."

"And you." He turned a side glance at her.

"I know of no royalty named Lydia."

"No," Stephen agreed. "But Lydia is a prosperous place filled with royalty and rich in resources. So, it's still fitting of you."

Lydia thought back to the first time she met Stephen. He remarked about her name, but they were interrupted before she could ask him to explain. She knew her name to be adapted from the distant place, but she knew little about it. In all her years in Nazareth, no one ever compared her to royalty and riches. Many equated her to the opposite.

The two chatted through the streets of Jerusalem while Jude and Arava gestured back and forth behind them.

"Here we are," Stephen announced as they hesitated outside a simple stone building. "The synagogue of the Freedmen."

Lydia took in the structure. It seemed like every other synagogue she'd seen. In fact, it looked like every other simple structure in Jerusalem. Why did Stephen seem so proud of it?

Stephen led them inside and moved to introduce Jude to the Rabbi.

Lydia stood next to Arava, waiting to find a seat among the women. With little to say to her new sister-in-law, she searched the gathering for any familiar faces. One headed in her direction.

"Shalom." Junia greeted Lydia with a kiss on her cheek. "I didn't know you were attending our synagogue today."

"Stephen invited me."

"Oh," Junia nodded. "Oh!" Realization dawned on her face. "I'm so happy you accepted his invitation. I can introduce you to his mother."

Fluttering returned to Lydia's stomach. "I think Stephen wanted to do the honors."

"Nonsense." She waved her off and grabbed her hand. "He's busy with the Rabbi. I can make the introductions."

Lydia stumbled under Junia's pull toward a group of women.

"Orpah," Junia called as she approached an older woman. "I have someone I'd like you to meet."

The woman turned from the others.

Junia stopped next to her but didn't release her hold on Lydia. "This is Lydia bat Joseph. Stephen invited her."

Orpah looked deep into Lydia's eyes.

It was then that Lydia discovered from whom Stephen had received his unique coloring. Orpah had the same ginger tea eyes as her son.

"Shalom, Lydia," Orpah said with a wide smile. "I'm glad you've joined us today."

Not trusting her words yet, Lydia simply bowed

toward the older woman.

Orpah leaned around Lydia. "And who else do we have?"

Lydia turned slightly to set eyes on her sister-in-law. She'd almost forgotten about her. "This is…" her introduction trailed off as she watched Arava's eyes dart wildly around the room.

The younger woman pulled her headscarf tight around her face and looked as though she were a fawn caught in a hunting party.

Lydia faltered to think of a single gesture to ask Arava what troubled her. Salome had warned her that Arava's ability to read lips was limited. She wondered, in the girl's frightened state, if she could even detect Lydia's attempts at communicating.

"The poor thing looks frightened," Orpah commented. "And she looks familiar."

Lydia took hold of Arava and forced her to look her in the eyes. With everything in her, she wanted to discover the source of her sister-in-law's fear and attempt to ease it.

Arava struggled against Lydia, grunting low.

"What is it?" Lydia whispered, knowing volume would not increase her chance of being understood.

Arava's gaze continued to dash around the room in a panic.

The rabbi called for the group's attention to start the meeting.

Lydia saw Jude and Stephen take their place among the men. With no other option, she guided Arava to a spot near Orpah and Junia.

Arava huddled into Lydia's side and concealed her face with her head wrap.

Allowing the younger woman to seek refuge in her presence, Lydia prayed for Adonai's wisdom.

As prayers were recited and songs sung, Lydia kept her seat, acting as a shield for whatever unseen danger was causing Arava to quake. She kept turning her attention to Stephen and Jude with silent pleas for them to see the unusual situation and come to her aid.

It wasn't until the rabbi introduced the special speaker that the invisible veil was lifted from Lydia's eyes.

Stepping up to the bema was none other than Saul, Arava's older brother.

Lydia's heart slammed against her chest, stealing her steady breath. Her eyes carefully searched the crowd. On the bottom step of the men's side sat Chislon. Saul's father carried a smirk of pride across his face.

Lydia didn't know if the man who'd shunned his daughter had laid eyes on either of them yet. Her gaze continued around the room, ever careful not to draw attention to herself. She discovered Saul's mother and sisters sitting near the bottom step of the women's side.

With gentle movements, Lydia wrapped her arm around Arava, pulling her as close as possible against herself. *What am I going to do, Adonai? What will happen if they see Arava?*

Saul wore a white and black head covering with extended borders and extremely long fringes that swayed with his steps. Leather straps of a phylactery wound around his left arm, starting at his hand, and climbed upward until they disappeared under his tunic.

There was no mistaking the official garb of a Pharisee.

He cleared his throat and read his selected text from the scroll that had been presented to him.

Lydia could barely listen as she prayed Adonai would hide Arava from her brother's sight.

With the tone and rhythm of a practiced Pharisee, Saul began to teach. He started by expounding on his reading, but his speech quickly turned to a call to guard their traditions at all costs.

"There are many we previously counted among us who have traded our way of life for another." Saul sat a little straighter in the bema seat. "Those who have chosen to follow this," he twirled his hand at his wrist in a dismissive manner, "other way. Adonai will deal with such."

His piercing gaze finally penetrated the wall Lydia had built around herself.

Saul hesitated. He templed his fingers in front of his mouth, keeping his eyes on her. He tapped his fingers on his lips several times before folding his hands in his lap. "We have laws to deal with those who blaspheme the name of our God. And we should not withhold judgment on those who seek to destroy our traditions."

He lifted a brow and leaned closer in her direction. "No one will escape the coming judgment." He settled back and continued with his warnings, bolstered by the crowd's verbal agreements.

For a single moment, Lydia was grateful Arava could not hear her brother's words. She was nearly jealous of her sister-in-law's deafness. The daggers of Saul's veiled threats found their mark true enough in her own soul.

The moment his speech was complete and the words of the last prayer were spoken, Lydia forced Arava to her feet and ushered her from the synagogue without so much as a backward glance in search of Jude or Stephen.

CHAPTER 12

In the month that followed, Lydia refused to speak of her visit to Stephen's synagogue while Arava retreated into Jude's arms.

Hadassah's dedication was the first time Lydia stepped foot into the city, fearing Saul's threats and the chance of having to face a disappointed Stephen. While the streets were still crowded, they had lightened in the weeks of her self-induced seclusion. The approaching Feast of Weeks would usher many visitors out of Jerusalem until the Feast of Tabernacles months later.

Lydia once more found herself waiting in the Court of Women as her niece was brought before the priests to be purchased back from Adonai.

Blood for blood. The voice whispered into her soul, sending chills down her back.

"Lydia."

The familiar sound of her name caused her body to tense. She closed her eyes, but she knew the voice would only repeat her name if she ignored it. Slowly, she opened her eyes and turned to face Stephen.

"I've been so worried about you."

Stephen approached a little too closely for Lydia's comfort, causing her to take a step back. "I've been busy."

"Jude explained everything." He hung his head.

"I'm so sorry."

Lydia wondered what choice words her brother had for Stephen after being forced to listen to Saul's speech. She hadn't dared bring up the topic with Jude. He frequently verbally battled Saul, rescued Arava from the viper's den of her family, and even received lashes for teaching about Jesus in the Temple all because of Saul's hatred of the Way. Having been able to keep his distance for several months, the endurance of being trapped in a room listening to Saul's rants and vague threats must have taken their toll on her brother.

Stephen raised his arms and dropped them against his sides. "You must believe that I did not know."

Lydia lifted her chin. She wasn't sure if she believed him, but he certainly seemed remorseful.

"Can you ever forgive me?" He held her gaze. "If I had known about the situation between Saul and his sister, I would not have insisted on your visit. I simply wanted to…" his explanation dissolved into a low mumble. He rubbed at the back of his neck. "All I wanted was for you to meet my family and take part in our worship. I fear I've made a mess of my attempts to…" He fumbled again for words.

Her frustration grew at his ramblings. "Speak plainly."

"I want to marry you, Lydia."

Stephen's declaration caused her to take another step back. She did not believe her hearing and shook her head to clear away whatever had sparked the wonderfully unattainable idea. "You what?"

"I want to marry you." His ginger eyes pleaded as

he held his ground. "I've spoken to James several times. It was his idea to invite you to the synagogue, though I don't think he knew that Saul's family were members. Oh, Lydia, nothing would bring me greater honor than for you to be my bride."

His words came forth like a rushing stream, threatening to carry her away. Lydia's eyes burned. "I can't marry you."

"James made no indication you had another seeker." Stephen shook his head and cleared the space between them. "He's done nothing but encourage my pursuit of you."

She held up her hands to keep him from moving closer. "I'm too plain and ordinary for a man like you. I could never bring you the joy you deserve."

"Lydia," he spoke her name with tenderness. "I am a plain man with little to offer the sister of Messiah, but that doesn't stop my desire to try."

Lydia's heart pounded against her chest. "I can't marry you." She picked up the hem of her worn tunic and fled back to the villa.

On the other side of the large villa door, she allowed tears to fall and made her way to the outer courtyard. Among her loyal friends, she poured out her soul.

Boaz's warm nuzzles and the playful romps of Esau and Jacob comforted her broken heart. By the time tears dried on her cheeks, she'd soaked in the healing balm the animals provided without a spoken word needed.

Familiar *kraas* of Elijah drew her attention. The

uniquely painted raven circled above before landing on the edge of the wooden railing.

Lydia rose from the straw to greet her friend with a few strokes on his gray chest. "It's too bad your wings are not strong enough to carry me far from here, Elijah."

After making sure each animal's needs had been met, Lydia reluctantly ventured inside. The house was quiet, except for the distant sounds of preparations coming from the kitchen. Upon entering, Lydia found Ria and Zipporah hard at work.

"Oh." Zipporah halted her kneading. "I didn't realize you had returned."

Lydia's cheeks warmed. "It's only me. I don't think the others have made it back yet."

Ria came close. "Are you well?" she whispered.

Lydia closed her eyes and gave her head a slight shake.

"Why don't you come assist me?" Ria spoke in a louder tone and motioned to Zipporah with a dip of her head.

Lydia nodded.

Outside the kitchen, Ria continued in a lower tone, "What happened?"

Fresh tears blurred Lydia's vision. "He asked me to marry him."

"Stephen?" Ria shouted.

Lydia looked over her shoulder toward the kitchen.

"Oh!" Ria clasped her hands over her own mouth. "I'm sorry," she mumbled through her fingers. She dropped her hands. "Lydia, that's wonderful."

"I declined."

Ria pulled her further away from the kitchen. "How could you deny such a man?"

Lydia lifted a shoulder. "He could never be happy with me. I'm not worthy."

"Lydia—" A loud knock on the door interrupted Ria's words. She huffed. "I'll see to it."

Lydia stood by, drying her tears on her head wrap.

Ria moved to open the door.

A man filled the entryway. "I'm looking for James ben Joseph."

Lydia recognized the broken Aramaic and rushed toward the door. "Barnabas?"

He dipped his head.

"Has something happened to Ananias?"

"No, no." Barnabas waved his hands toward her. "Ananias is well. He send me." He reached into his satchel and produced a small scroll.

Lydia accepted the papyrus and unrolled it to read the message contained within.

Ananias, a follower of the Way, greetings to James ben Joseph and all those in the house of Theodotus.

We've heard of the work in Jerusalem and all that Adonai has done since the days we were among you.

I've sent Barnabas to you, seeking aid for the Way Followers in Damascus. Many have come to believe in Jesus as Messiah and that choice has cost them greatly. We pray that any help you are willing to send will be multiplied in the hands of Adonai. Pray for us as we continue to reach others with the teachings of Jesus.

All those in Damascus greet you.

Lydia re-rolled the scroll. "My brother and the others should return soon from the Temple. Please come in."

Barnabas accepted the offer and entered further into the entryway.

"Zipporah is in the kitchen." Lydia tucked the scroll into her tunic. "I'm sure she can find you something to eat while you wait."

Barnabas bowed his head and headed for the kitchen.

"Lydia, you've got to find Stephen," Ria picked up their previous conversation as if they'd not been interrupted. "Tell him you were mistaken, and you want to marry him."

Lydia put her hands up to her face. "I can't."

"But—"

"Let this be, Ria," Lydia warned.

Ria huffed off toward the kitchen.

The door swung open. James and the others poured forth.

"Lydia," James' tone held a sharp edge. "We've been through half the city looking for you. Why did you leave the Temple before the ceremony was complete?"

The others encircled her, waiting for an explanation.

"I-I-I," she stammered. "I have word from Ananias." She retrieved the scroll and held it out to James.

He snatched the parchment and read it quickly. Reaching the bottom of the message, he lifted an eyebrow at her. "Barnabas is here?"

"In the kitchen." She gestured toward the back of the house. "Getting some food."

"I will see to our guest." James rolled up the scroll. "But I want to have a word with you afterward."

Lydia swallowed past the rising lump in her throat and managed a simple nod in agreement.

James retreated to the kitchen.

The others dispersed through the house. All except Assia, who stood holding Hadassah and staring at Lydia.

She caught her sister's awkward glare. "What?"

"What did Stephen say to you?"

Lydia flinched. "What?"

"I saw him, the man they call Stephen." She took a step forward. "He was speaking with you in the courtyard."

"I don't know what you're talking about."

"Lydia bat Joseph," her tone echoed their mother's, "speak truth to me."

The lump in Lydia's throat turned to pure acid.

CHAPTER 13

"Stephen revealed his intention to marry me," Lydia spoke through the burn, "but I turned him away."

"Why would you do that?" Assia rocked the babe in her arms. "From everything I've heard about him, he seems to be quite an agreeable match."

"He's wonderful." The man's ginger eyes flashed in her mind. She shook them away. "That's the problem. He's too wonderful for me."

"What makes you say that?"

"Look at me." She held up the ends of her worn tunic. "I'm as plain as they come. I'm not humble like Ima. I'm not as beautiful as you and Salome."

"Lydia," Assia put a soft hand on her sister's cheek, "you are beautiful and as hard-working and dedicated as any. You simply can't see what Stephen and the rest of us see." She dropped her hand and then her gaze to her daughter. "What I hope Hadassah sees one day."

"What?"

"Worth, sister." She lifted her gaze. "You are worthy, even when you don't see it in yourself."

Lydia turned away.

"But if you truly don't see a life here in Jerusalem," Assia continued, "you can always return home to Nazareth with me."

"Nazareth?" The name slipped off Lydia's tongue

like a foreign word. She'd not only distanced herself physically from the tiny village of her birth, but mentally as well in the last several months. *Nothing good comes from Nazareth.* Saul's hate-filled words caught fire again in her soul. "There's nothing there for me."

"Lydia," James' stern call bounced off the stone walls.

Lydia looked up to see him waiting by the inner courtyard. She flicked a glance at Assia.

Assia gave a simple nod and moved to leave.

With heavy steps, Lydia made her way to James' side.

"Walk with me." James set a steady pace around the indoor space.

Lydia kept her mouth closed, waiting for her brother's forthcoming speech.

"I need your help to understand something," James' tone cooled. "For weeks, I've been encouraging Stephen's interest in you and now I hear you've turned down his offer of marriage."

Lydia's cheeks flamed. How many conversations had occurred between her brother and Stephen about her?

"Stephen is a good man. A fine man. A man who has displayed excellent morals." James folded his hands behind his back. "Yet you, a woman who has had no previous offers, turn away his attention."

The fire in Lydia's face reached down her neck. So, it was true. No man had ever sought her for marriage.

"I come out of the Priest's Courtyard to find

Stephen standing there, looking as if someone had ripped his beard from his chin." James clicked his tongue.

The image her brother painted of Stephen's hurt pierced through Lydia. She never intended to cause him pain.

"I know the trip to his synagogue was less than ideal," James continued, "but you can't lay that blame at Stephen's feet. He did not know the tension between our family and Saul's. Arava is safe with us and no harm has come of it." He sat on the stone bench and patted the empty seat next to him. "So, tell me, what has caused you to deny Stephen?"

Lydia crumbled onto the bench, fighting tears that begged for release. "How can I accept his offer?" her voice cracked. "Stephen has shown me nothing but kindness, yet I have nothing to give him in return."

"You have yourself." James wrapped his arm around her. "That is more than enough."

Pressing into her brother's side, Lydia released her tears. The sound of someone clearing their throat caused Lydia to jerk her head up.

Stephen stood about a stone's throw away, clutching a bag.

"Stephen." James rose to greet the man and looked at Lydia. "I'm sure you two have much to discuss."

"Please stay," Stephen requested. "I want to do this right this time." He stepped toward Lydia, holding out the bag. "I know I'm not a perfect man. I'm not even a good man. But I care a great deal for you, Lydia. If you would reconsider my offer, I would spend every day of my life showing you just how much you've come to mean to me." He pushed the bag toward her.

Fresh streams cascaded down Lydia's face. "What's this?"

"I'm hoping it's a gift of promise for our betrothal." His cheeks shifted to pink.

With shaking hands, Lydia reached for the bag and opened the top. Blue material peeked out of the satchel. "I don't understand."

"Take it out."

Lydia reached in and removed the material that unfolded into a new dress. She dropped the bag, holding the beautiful blue dress upward. The linen was crisp and clean. "It's lovely."

"It's yours." His smile brightened. "All yours."

Lydia fingered the material and crushed it against her chest. "A dress just for me." She held the garment to her face and inhaled its fresh scent.

"It might be the only new garment for a long time." Stephen chuckled. "I remembered how much you admired it that day in the market. I couldn't think of a better betrothal gift."

She peered at him over the dress, noticing how his bright ginger eyes shone over his wide grin. Those same eyes had invaded her dreams and her thoughts for weeks. Slowly lowering the garment, she said, "I accept."

"Truly?" He stepped to clear the space, but hesitated.

"Truly."

James embraced Stephen. "I'm glad to be the first

to welcome you into the family, my friend." He gave his sister a wink. "I'll inform Rabbi Ethan, and we'll arrange an official ceremony. I'm sure Ima will be pleased to hear we are adding another son to the family."

"I should go," Stephen admitted. "There are many plans to make."

"I'll see you out," James offered.

Lydia clutched the new dress to her chest and then held it up again. The gorgeous blue held hints of purple, revealing it was most likely dyed with glastum. She'd never seen a more beautiful garment. With quick steps, she hurried upstairs to try it on.

Inside the privacy of an upper room, she shrugged out of her undyed wool dress and slipped the new one over her under tunic. It fit her better than any of Assia's old dresses, and only needed a few adjustments to make it perfect.

She retrieved her polished bronze and held it out to arm's length. "I can't wait to show Naavah and Junia." She moved the mirror around, trying to get a better look.

"I see you accepted Stephen's offer." Assia filled the doorway, her arms vacant of baby Hadassah. "Well, turn around. Let me get a good look."

Obeying, Lydia spun in a slow circle.

"It's truly your color," she admitted. "I think Stephen will make you very happy."

Lydia held the metal mirror to her chest. "I pray I can make him happy, too."

A few days later, Lydia wore her new dress to Rabbi

Ethan's synagogue. She and Stephen exchanged vows before Adonai and their families. Lydia couldn't help getting lost in Stephen's ginger eyes as she committed to being his and soaked in his promises to care for her all the days of his life.

Back at the villa, Theodotus requested a small feast prepared to honor the new couple.

Laughter filled the air late into the night.

Lydia tucked each moment into her soul, bathing herself in the pureness of joy.

The following morning, she kissed Assia's cheeks as the family of three gathered with a caravan heading out of Jerusalem.

Lydia held onto Hadassah a few moments longer. Rubbing her nose into her niece's neck, she whispered promises of reunion and prayers of blessings. When she could not hold on to her any longer, she released the girl back into her mother's arms and kissed Assia's cheeks once more. "Safe travels."

"Promise to send word as soon as the two of you are wed," Assia requested.

"I will," Lydia promised.

The rest of the family shared their well wishes and exchanged promises of future messages. All too soon, the caravan set off toward the north, carrying Assia, Hiskiel, and Hadassah back to Nazareth.

Lydia watched until the dust settled, praying for her sister and the family that had grown before her eyes. How long before it would be her turn to hold a baby in her aching arms? Maybe one with ginger eyes.

CHAPTER 14

Winter rains once more gave way to the citrus harvest, and the late rains produced an abundant crop of barley and flax.

The villa, which started to feel small to Lydia among the new arrivals from Galilee, hummed with a constant flow of activity from sunrise to the setting of the same. Women cared for little ones and chores, while the men spent their days in the city teaching, healing, and caring for the needy of Jerusalem.

Many of the disciples decided to move their families into other dwellings in the city, providing more space in the large villa.

Lydia often missed the extra hands that made chores lighter. Though she couldn't fault the families for wanting more space. Those who remained still eased the load of her family and the house servants. Several of the women continued to visit to help in any way they could.

Naavah eventually joined their collection of women when Joseph finally found the courage to betroth the former adulteress.

Lydia beamed when the couple announced their intentions to the family.

"If Jesus can forgive her," Joseph declared with a fiery gaze, "that's good enough for me."

The woman, who'd been trapped by the Pharisee and her previous husband all those years ago, blushed under the tender attention of Joseph.

Lydia, who'd been patiently awaiting her own wedding feast that was set to take place after Passover, offered an idea. "Why not share our wedding feasts?"

Naavah embraced her and the offer with open arms.

Stephen had asked Lydia to wait a traditional year so he could make proper preparations for their life together. She reluctantly agreed, all the while secretly desiring to be his as soon as possible. The request opened the door to celebrate two marriages for the cost of one. A blessing that was not easily overlooked by the simple family stretching every coin that passed through their hands.

With Passover fast approaching, the upcoming double wedding feast consumed Lydia's thoughts. She held baby Joshua on her hip in the kitchen, giving the growing boy a wooden spoon to chew on while she attempted kneading dough with her other hand. A feat she was failing to accomplish.

Every time she pressed into the dough, Joshua showed his displeasure of the movement with a yank of her hair or a cry for attention. How had her mother always made taking care of little ones and managing everything else look effortless? Mary raised seven children with help only from the occasional relative. Lydia helped care for Simon and Salome but with much of the weight laid on her mother and Assia. Lydia couldn't accomplish caring for one child alone for a few hours while getting bread in the oven.

Arava appeared next to her and pointed to Joshua.

Lydia nodded. As much as she wanted the diversion, holding the squirming boy and making food was no simple task. She eased Joshua into Arava's open arms.

Her silent sister-in-law happily took the young child into another room to amuse him.

With both hands free, Lydia finished making bread and searched for her next task. A hunt that was interrupted by Junia bursting into the villa with a tiny bundle cradled against her chest.

"Help!" She hurried toward Lydia.

"What's happened?"

"Are any of the men here?"

Lydia pointed upstairs. "Stephen is praying in the upper room."

Without explanation, Junia flew up the stone steps.

Lydia trailed behind her and entered the room only moments after Junia.

"Please, Stephen," Junia pleaded. "You might be her only hope."

Stephen accepted the wrapped object into his hands and pulled away the fabric.

Lydia moved close enough to see a small infant nestled in the linen. The girl was pale as a ship's sail, and her breathing sounded forced. "Who is she?"

Junia turned a wide glare at Lydia but didn't respond.

Stephen rested his hand on the child's head and looked at the ceiling. "Adonai, if it be Your will, restore this child and make her whole again. Breathe Your life into her so that she may testify of Your goodness all the days of her life."

The room was still for several heartbeats until the tiny cry of the girl broke through the quiet.

"Praise Adonai!" Junia shouted and clapped her hands.

It wasn't the first time Lydia witnessed her betrothed be used as a vessel for Adonai's healing. In the months since he took on the mantle of the seven, Stephen performed a great number of healings, including driving out demons and restoring health to those near the gates of Sheol. Lydia observed several of the miraculous events, but each one held her in awe.

Stephen gently handed the girl back to Junia.

As the baby moved from one set of hands to the other, Lydia noticed the girl's complexion shifted to a completely normal tone, and her breathing was steady. "Who is she?" she repeated.

"She's a rock child," Junia said simply, as if there was no need to explain further.

"A what?"

"It's a common practice among Roman mothers to abandon their unwanted children, mostly girls," she held the girl against her chest, "out on the rocks and allow the Fates to decide their future."

"That's awful."

"That's just the way of it," Junia said with a shrug. She stared into the face of the little girl. "In a strange way, it reminds me of my place among Adonai's people."

"How so?"

"While the Jews may be blood children of Abraham," she glanced up at Lydia, "Adonai has adopted us Gentiles as His own, too. In the eyes of a Roman, it's an even stronger bond."

"What makes you say that?"

"From a Roman perspective, they consider adopted children above even blood children. The bonds of adoption are so strong that not even the law can revoke their position. That's why many Roman families formally adopt their own children after they've seen their first harvest."

The practice sounded odd to Lydia, yet somehow beautiful. Did Adonai really view Gentiles as the Romans viewed adopted children?

She lifted onto her toes to look into the girl's tiny face. "What are you going to call her?"

Junia hummed to herself. "I've always liked the name Shamira."

"Protection," Lydia voiced the meaning. "Seems fitting, since Adonai sent you to rescue her from the short arms of the Roman gods."

"I think so."

The girl let out another cry.

"She must be hungry," Junia mused. "I don't know who I could use as a wet nurse."

A peculiar thought struck Lydia. "What about goat's milk?"

Junia twisted her nose. "Are you suggesting I have Shamira suckle at the teat of one of your goats?"

Lydia shook her head. "You can dip a cloth into a

cup of goat's milk and let her suck on it. There's some fresh milk in the kitchen."

"A strange idea, but it just may work." Junia nuzzled Shamira. "Let's go fill that belly." She departed the room with the baby.

Lydia turned toward Stephen. "I'm once again in awe of you, my beloved. Adonai certainly uses you in powerful ways."

"Adonai is powerful." Stephen tapped her nose. "I'm simply a willing vessel."

Lydia smiled. She couldn't wait until she would place a child into his arms.

"Speaking of willing," Stephen interrupted her thoughts. "I have something I'd like to discuss with you."

"Oh?"

"I received an invitation to speak at my synagogue, and I want you there with me when I do."

Lydia's heart slammed against her chest. The fear and dread of Saul and his threats washed over her as if she were hearing them for the first time. "How can you ask this of me?"

Stephen stepped closer and lowered his voice. "I know your family has issues with Saul. I wouldn't ask this if it wasn't important to me."

A tremor shook through Lydia.

"They've heard of what Adonai has been doing, and they want me to come and share about the work being done in His name."

Lydia stared into Stephen's pleading eyes. His voice and the calm of his presence soothed her warring heart.

"How can I turn down such an opportunity? It would mean the world to have you there when I step onto the bema and share about your brother."

She sucked in a breath. "As long as I can go alone this time, I will attend."

"I understand." He smiled his wide grin. "Once we are wed, we'll have to have a different conversation about where we will worship together."

A chill raced down her back. *I'll follow you anywhere, beloved. As long as it's not to the synagogue of the Freedman.*

CHAPTER 15

A few weeks later, Lydia shimmied into her blue dress. She took extra care to wash the new fabric, which had softened from the lye scrub.

With gentle strokes, she brushed her hair with Salome's comb and set a headcloth of her mother's properly into place. After applying scented oils to her neck, she gave one last glance to her reflection in her polished bronze. She wouldn't be the most beautiful woman in the synagogue, but she'd done what she could with what she had.

Stephen was waiting for her in the open area of the villa when she came down the stairs.

He smiled up at her, the act lighting his entire face. "You look lovely."

Lydia's cheeks warmed. "I'm sorry to keep you waiting."

"Not at all."

She flicked a glance to James, who'd been speaking with Stephen. The look on his face revealed the conversation had not been good news. "Is everything well?"

"I was simply updating Stephen on some issues." James shook his head. "Nothing to worry about."

"Well, I'm ready." Lydia adjusted her head covering.

"Then let us take our leave." Stephen bowed his head toward James. "I will see to those widows after the meeting."

James returned the acknowledgment with a bow to them both.

The walk to the synagogue gave Lydia a chance to review details with Stephen about their upcoming feast. With the plan to share the celebration with Joseph and Naavah, communication was of utmost importance.

"Naavah's brother is due to arrive in the coming days," Lydia shared with Stephen. "She invited him as a representative of her family. Though she was surprised he agreed to attend at all."

Stephen hummed in agreement.

"And my mother wanted to know if there are any special requests from your family regarding the food."

"I'm sure whatever Mary makes will be delicious."

"And, of course, the villa will be decorated."

"Hmm."

"Stephen?" Lydia stopped. "Are you well?"

He hesitated. "Why do you ask?"

"You seem… distracted."

"Forgive me." He held his head. "It's the weight of speaking today. I haven't read in front of a gathering since I was young."

"You are an excellent speaker." She longed to reach for him and provide physical comfort. With strict traditions in place as to contact before marriage, she had only her words to offer. "Adonai continues to rest His Spirit upon you, Stephen. You have nothing to fear."

"I'm sure you're right." He dropped his hand and his ginger eyes flashed at her. "I'm so glad you agreed to be present today."

I wouldn't want to be anywhere else but with you.

Lydia continued to share the feast details as they made their way to the synagogue. She was surprised at the enormous crowd who had turned out to hear Stephen speak. The small building was packed with people eager to hear from the one who'd been healing and driving out demons in Jerusalem.

She found Stephen's mother, Orpah, and settled into the crowd of women alongside her. Her heart sped up, searching for any signs of Saul and his family. She didn't see Saul's sisters or mother among the women, but Chislon sat on the bottom step of the men's side. To his right, Saul sat adorned in his Pharisee garb. His dark eyes fixed a wicked gaze on her.

Though tempted to return his threatening stare, Lydia let her gaze continue around the room, hoping to display more courage than she felt. With her eyes busy elsewhere, she couldn't shake the feeling Saul's glare remained transfixed on her.

The rabbi led the group in prayers and songs before introducing Stephen.

Lydia beamed at her beloved, watching him step onto the bema and read from the selected passage.

Stephen's voice was powerful and rang clear in the open space as he read the words of the prophet Isaiah.

When the scroll was returned to its place, Stephen took his seat on the bema and began to share about the power of Jesus of Nazareth.

Lydia listened intently as Stephen recounted many of the signs and wonders Jesus did during his years as a traveling teacher. She ignored the indistinct murmurs which floated among the crowd.

Stephen expounded on Jesus' arrest, conviction, and punishment as if he'd been witness to each.

Lydia's heart twisted at the mental images of her brother and the lonely hours he endured during his crucifixion. She'd been tucked away in Benjamin's home among her siblings as their oldest brother sacrificed himself. They'd been wholly unaware of Adonai's plan for His Messiah until it was far too late.

Lifting his voice and his eyes, Stephen shared about the glorious day when Jesus arose from his tomb and showed himself to his followers.

Lydia's heart lifted with the joy that flowed from her betrothed's conviction. He truly was an incredible speaker.

Murmurs shifted to disputes from the men's side.

"How can a man return from the dead?" someone asked.

"I assure you," Stephen turned toward the question, "Jesus holds power over death." He shifted his gaze to the gathering. "How many of you were there when Jesus called Lazarus from his tomb?"

Some lifted hands, while others chatted to one another.

"I can testify I was," Stephen answered his own question. "If Jesus can do that for a man, surely Adonai can do it for His Messiah."

One man rose to his feet. "We've heard Stephen speak blasphemous words against Moses and Adonai."

"I have spoken plainly among you," Stephen defended himself. "I've said only that which Adonai has pressed upon me."

"Jesus is not our Messiah," someone shouted.

Lydia's heart squeezed. Why couldn't they understand the truth?

"We've heard Jesus' claims to destroy the Temple," another added.

"Please." Stephen rose from the bema seat. "I intended no ill words, only truth." He continued sharing of the miraculous healings and the power he'd felt being able to drive out demons.

"He claims to have the power of Adonai!" a man shouted.

"Blasphemer!" someone else accused.

More shouts came from the men's side of the room.

Lydia watched Stephen frantically search the gathering.

"He is a blasphemer," someone repeated.

"Let's take him before the council," another suggested. "They will deal with his blasphemy."

"My friends," Stephen pleaded, "you know me. I am doing the work of Adonai. I'm only a vessel."

The crowd crashed over Stephen like a wave, dragging him out of the synagogue.

Lydia fought through the frantic crowd of women. She struggled to keep up with the men carrying Stephen away.

Several held onto Stephen's outer cloak as they ushered him through the streets toward the Temple.

Lydia's breath burned in her lungs, and her heart picked up its pace. She could barely keep her eyes on Stephen through the group of men.

They didn't slow as they ascended the white steps of the Temple. People moved aside as the throng pressed their way through the courts.

When they reached the Chamber of Hewn Stone, the men threw Stephen at the feet of Joseph ben Caiaphas. The same man who sentenced Jesus to die at the hands of Rome, sat in a shining white priestly robe.

Lydia pressed against the cool stone wall, hoping to hide herself from the eyes of the Sanhedrin.

The gathering of older men whispered among themselves on both sides of the semi-circled room.

Joseph peered down at Stephen. "Why has this man been brought before me?"

A few of the crowd from the synagogue stepped forward.

"High Priest Joseph," one spoke up, "this man never ceases to speak words against this holy place and the law."

Lydia clenched her jaw. She knew the words of the witness to be false, but she had no place to speak in the assembly. She hoped someone would speak honestly for her beloved.

"We've heard him say that Jesus of Nazareth will destroy this place and will change the customs that Moses delivered to us," another added.

Joseph set his gaze on Stephen.

With shaking legs, Stephen slowly rose to face his accusers.

Lydia fixed her attention on his ginger eyes, which appeared to shine brighter than she'd ever seen. Stephen's entire face seemed to shine like the midday sun.

Whispers grew louder as the words "holy messenger" lifted above others.

Never having seen a divine one of Adonai for herself, she wondered if her beloved was counted among men or the army of Adonai. The man she knew had done many wonders by the power of Adonai, but she also knew him to be a simple man. Surely, he was merely a man and no more.

CHAPTER 16

"Are these things so?" Joseph's voice echoed around the chamber.

Lydia kept her attention on Stephen.

He caught her eyes for only a moment before he turned his bright gaze to the men. "Brothers and fathers, hear me. The God of glory appeared to our father Abraham when he was in Mesopotamia, before he lived in Haran, and said to him, 'Go out from your land and from your kindred and go into the land that I will show you.'"

The private conversations ceased as Stephen's voice rose above the clamor. "Then Abraham went out from the land of the Chaldeans and lived in Haran. And after his father died, Adonai removed him from there into this land in which you are now living. Yet he gave him no inheritance in it, not even a foot's length, but promised to give it to him as a possession and to his offspring after him, though he had no child."

Lydia's heart twisted. She wanted nothing more than to run from the room, but Stephen's speech captivated her, along with the others.

"Adonai spoke to this effect," Stephen lifted one finger toward Joseph, "that his offspring would be sojourners in a land belonging to others, who would enslave them and afflict them four hundred years. 'But

I will judge the nation that they serve,' said Adonai, 'and after that they shall come out and worship me in this place.'"

Lydia heard the story of their father Abraham on countless occasions, but the story took on new life as it dripped from Stephen's lips.

"Adonai gave Abraham the covenant of circumcision," Stephen continued, allowing his gaze to pass over each man. "And so, Abraham became the father of Isaac, and circumcised him on the eighth day, and Isaac became the father of Jacob, and Jacob of the twelve patriarchs. And the patriarchs, jealous of Joseph, sold him into Egypt; but Adonai was with him and rescued him out of all his afflictions and gave him favor and wisdom before Pharaoh, who made him ruler over Egypt and over all his household."

Lydia dared a peek at the council members.

The group of seventy men was transfixed on Stephen.

She returned her attention to her beloved as he recounted the well-known story of their shared past.

"There came a famine throughout all Egypt and Canaan, and great affliction, and our fathers could find no food. But when Jacob heard that there was grain in Egypt, he sent out our fathers on their first visit. And on the second visit," Stephen held up two fingers, "Joseph made himself known to his brothers, and Joseph's family became known to Pharaoh. Joseph sent and summoned Jacob his father and all his kindred, seventy-five persons in all."

Lifting herself away from the wall, Lydia edged

closer. Stephen's words pulled her in as much as they were the rest of the gathering. His face beamed as bright as the Temple lampstands.

"Jacob went down into Egypt, and he died." Stephen turned around to address the other side of the room. "He and our fathers, and they were carried back to Shechem and laid in the tomb that Abraham had bought for a sum of silver from the sons of Hamor in Shechem. But as the time of the promise drew near, which Adonai had granted to Abraham, the people increased and multiplied in Egypt until there arose over Egypt another king who did not know Joseph."

Lydia took another step closer.

"This new king dealt shrewdly with our race and forced our fathers to expose their infants, so that they would not be kept alive." Stephen caught sight of Lydia. "At this time Moses was born; and he was beautiful in Adonai's sight. He was brought up for three months in his father's house, and when he was exposed, Pharaoh's daughter adopted him and brought him up as her own son."

A flash of ginger eyes appeared in Lydia's mind. She dreamt of Stephen's child for over a year. He was as real to her as baby Moses had been in her childhood lessons. She dared another step toward her beloved, but he gave her a warning glare.

"Moses was instructed in all the wisdom of the Egyptians, and he was mighty in his words and deeds." Stephen faced Joseph. "When he was forty years old, it came into his heart to visit his brothers, the children of Israel. Seeing one of them being wronged, he defended the oppressed man and avenged him by striking down the Egyptian." He paused as he looked over the collection again. "He supposed his brothers would understand that Adonai was giving them salvation by his hand, but they did not understand. On the following day, he appeared to them as they were quarreling and tried to reconcile them, saying, 'Men, you are brothers. Why do you wrong each other?' But the man who was wronging his neighbor thrust him aside, saying, 'Who made you a ruler and a judge over us? Do you want to kill me as you killed the Egyptian yesterday?' At this retort Moses fled and became an exile in the land of Midian, where he became the father of two sons."

Stephen raised his arms above his head. "Now when forty years passed, an angel appeared to him in the wilderness of Mount Sinai, in a flame of fire in a bush. When Moses saw it, he was amazed at the sight, and as he drew near to look, there came the voice of Adonai: 'I am the God of your fathers, the God of Abraham and of Isaac and of Jacob.' And Moses trembled and did not dare to look."

He dropped his hands. "Then the Lord said to him, 'Take off the sandals from your feet, for the place where you are standing is holy ground. I have surely seen the affliction of my people who are in Egypt, and have heard their groaning, and I have come down to deliver them. And now come, I will send you to Egypt.'"

The familiar story washed fresh over Lydia as Adonai's spirit spoke boldly from Stephen's mouth.

"This Moses, whom they rejected, saying, 'Who made you a ruler and a judge?'—this man Adonai sent as both ruler and redeemer by the hand of the angel who appeared to him in the bush." Stephen raised one arm out as if holding a staff. "This man led them out, performing wonders and signs in Egypt and at the Red Sea and in the wilderness for forty years. This is the Moses who said to the Israelites, 'Adonai will raise up for you a prophet like me from your brothers.'"

He stepped toward the council. "This is the one who was in the congregation in the wilderness with the angel who spoke to him at Mount Sinai, and with our fathers. He received living oracles to give to us. Our fathers refused to obey him, but thrust him aside, and in their hearts, they turned to Egypt, saying to Aaron, 'Make for us gods who will go before us. As for this Moses who led us out from the land of Egypt, we do not know what has become of him.'"

He moved to the other side of the room. "They made a golden calf, and offered a sacrifice to the idol and were rejoicing in the works of their hands. But Adonai turned away and gave them over to worship the host of heaven, as it is written in the book of the prophets: 'Did you bring to me slain beasts and sacrifices, during the forty years in the wilderness, O house of Israel? You took up the tent of Moloch and the star of your god Rephan, the images that you made to worship; and I will send you into exile beyond Babylon.'"

Stephen walked slowly back toward Joseph. "Our fathers had the tent of witness in the wilderness, just as he who spoke to Moses directed him to make it, according to the pattern that he had seen. Our fathers in turn brought it in with Joshua when they dispossessed the nations that Adonai drove out before our fathers. So, it was until the days of David, who found favor in the sight of Adonai and asked to find a dwelling place for the God of Jacob. But it was Solomon who built a house for him."

He bowed his head. "Yet the Most High does not dwell in houses made by hands, as the prophet says, 'Heaven is my throne, and the earth is my footstool. What kind of house will you build for me, says the Lord, or what is the place of my rest? Did not my hand make all these things?'" He raised his gaze, setting it on Joseph. "You stiff-necked people, uncircumcised in heart and ears, you always resist the Holy Spirit. As your fathers did, so do you. Which of the prophets did your fathers not persecute? They killed those who announced beforehand the coming of the Righteous One, whom you have now betrayed and murdered, you who received the law as delivered by angels and did not keep it."

CHAPTER 17

Lydia's heart pounded against her chest. Surely, with all Stephen shared about Moses, Joseph would see that he was a just man who had not blasphemed Adonai. Would the High Priest see through the false witnesses and proclaim Stephen innocent?

Joseph templed his fingers to his lips for several seconds. "You want us to keep the law?" He folded his hands and placed them in his lap. "Then it shall judge you." He flicked his chin to the crowd.

The men surrounding Stephen took hold of him, pressing him out of the chamber and into the Temple courtyard.

Lydia hurried after them, shouting, "Stephen!"

Fighting against their hold, Stephen searched around, then lifted his gaze.

Lydia watched as he noticed something above them. She, too, lifted her gaze to search for what had drawn his attention.

"Look!" Stephen shouted, pointing to the clouds overhead. "I see the heavens opened, and the Son of Man standing at the right hand of Adonai."

The people surrounding them cried out against his claims.

"Blasphemy!"

They pounded their chests and pulled at their

tunics.

"Blasphemy!"

They dug at their ears.

Stephen raised his arms toward the sky. "I see Jesus."

Straining to see the same, Lydia searched for her brother's face among the wisps of white. Only the blue of the sky stared back at her. She dropped her gaze to Stephen once again. His face shone brightly, reminding her of the stories of Moses after he'd been on Mount Sinai in the presence of Adonai. She wondered if Stephen really was looking into the place where Adonai dwelled.

"I see Him." Stephen's bottom lip quivered. "Jesus is standing at the right hand of Adonai."

The men shoved Stephen out of the courtyard and down the Temple stairs.

Lydia lifted the ends of her blue dress to hurry down the broad steps of the Inspection Gate. Her toes caught on a step, causing her to tumble forward. Before hitting the stone, she steadied herself on a woman heading in the opposite direction. With no time to apologize, Lydia pushed off the stranger and cleared the rest of the staircase.

The crowd drove Stephen down into the Kidron Valley.

Following them through the sands, Lydia saw Saul about a stone's throw away. He waited near a pit regaled in his full Pharisee attire.

As the multitude approached, Saul glanced at Stephen, who was still shouting about Jesus. "You have all heard this man's blasphemous words." He set dark eyes on Lydia.

His piercing gaze sent daggers deep into her soul.

Saul lifted his voice, "By the law of Moses, we are required to stone such men."

Those gathered around tore off their outer cloaks and deposited them at Saul's feet. They picked up stones and encircled Stephen, trapping him like a wild animal.

Walking backward, Stephen tripped and stumbled as they closed in around him.

Lydia rushed toward Saul. "You can stop this," she pleaded. "As a Pharisee, you have the authority."

Saul stood over the cloaks like a Roman statue standing guard over an altar. He gave no answer to her pleas and showed no motivation to move from his position.

When the men came to the pit, they pushed Stephen in and hurled their rocks in his direction.

The first caught Stephen's cheek, leaving a sizable gash. The next hit his midsection, causing him to double over. A third slammed into his head, causing him to cover his face in defense.

Lydia pulled at her hair as the rocks continued to rain down on Stephen. She cleared the space between herself and Saul. "You filthy Pharisee. Too holy to soil your hands, but willing to stoke the fires of bloodlust." She stepped as close to Saul as she dared. "Stop this madness. Stop it," her demands bordered on shrieks.

Saul's lips slid into a sly grin. "Blasphemy is punishable by death."

Lydia watched as his dark eyes flamed with hunger; a hunger she realized would only be satisfied with the blood of her betrothed. She turned to see more rocks fall upon Stephen.

He took blow after blow as blood trickled from marks on his face and hands. He raised his arms and shouted, "Lord Jesus, receive my spirit!"

Lydia looked up into the sky. "If you're truly there, Jesus, stop this." She lowered her gaze to catch sight of Stephen. "Please."

Stephen was barely visible beyond the growing pile of stones.

For only a single moment, she caught his gaze.

He slowly lifted his eyes toward the sky. "Lord, do not hold this sin against them." He closed his eyes, accepting his fate, as more rocks covered his face.

"No!" Lydia rushed down into the pit.

The last few stones caught her as she threw herself onto the pile. "Stephen!"

The sand near the rocks turned a deep red.

"Stephen!" She clawed at the stoney hill, ripping her fingernails in the process. She cursed Saul as she recalled the day in the market in which Stephen had stepped between her and Saul. He had defended her against Saul, but today she couldn't do the same for him.

"Stephen," her betrothed's name came in quick sobs. "Oh, Stephen." She shoved rock after rock away while the sounds of retreating footsteps filled the valley.

As the rocks shifted, she saw Stephen's lifeless

body.

Hands appeared near her. She turned to see the six men who had served beside Stephen over the last year work to remove the larger stones she couldn't move.

With their help, the pile was cleared from Stephen, but it was too late. His body lay curled and crushed under the weight of the stoning.

Lydia crumbled beside him, reaching to caress his lips with her bloody fingertips. She longed to kiss them from the moment she gave her heart to him. Now, his lips would remain forever out of her reach, along with the life he promised her.

She pulled his limp body into her lap and rocked him as she would a child. "Oh, Stephen," she wailed.

Red tinted her vision. Marks covered Stephen's face and the rest of his exposed skin. Blood stained his tunic. The sand under them was soaked with the liquid of his life. A faint metallic scent drifted toward her mixing with Stephen's familiar scent of cedar.

Flames of anger licked her cheeks. It was more than she could bear. She set her face to the sky. "You could've stopped this." Hot tears poured down her face. "He trusted you. He said he saw you standing there. Yet, you did nothing."

The six men stood around her, weeping and crying out. Their laments filled the valley until they could weep no more.

Lydia added her wails to the songs of sorrow. She yelled and cried until her throat burned. Her midsection ached and her chest felt heavy. Laying her cheek next to Stephen's, she allowed her tears to fall on his face.

A psalm of David flooded her mind. She opened her mouth and sang, "How long, O Lord? Will You forget me forever? How long will You hide your face from me? How long must I take counsel in my soul and have sorrow in my heart all the day?" Saul's malicious grin painted her vision while the next lines poured forth, "How long shall my enemy be exalted over me? Consider and answer me, O Lord my God; light up my eyes, lest I sleep the sleep of death, lest my enemy say, 'I have prevailed over him,' lest my foes rejoice because I am shaken."

She paused. The next words caught in her throat. She couldn't bring herself to repeat David's statement of faith in Adonai's steadfast love. Gazing down at the frozen face of her betrothed, she felt none of Adonai's love.

In the growing silence of the valley, one of the men knelt beside her. "We must bury him."

Lydia crushed Stephen's body against her chest. "You can't have him."

"Lydia," the man spoke her name slowly. "Evening is coming. We must prepare him."

She looked up to see the man called Nicolaus through blurred vision. "Our wedding feast is in a month." Fresh sobs broke through. "We are to be married."

"I know." Nicolaus hung his head. "Please, let us take him."

Lydia's gaze fell to Stephen's open eyes. Those ginger eyes she fell in love with stared back at her without the spark they once held. She brushed some hair away from his face.

"Lydia, please," Nicolaus begged.

She rocked Stephen's body back and forth. "You can't have him," she whispered.

Red mingled with the blue of the dress Stephen gave her as a promise of their pending marriage feast. The blood of her betrothed marred the once beautiful garment.

"You just stood there," she spoke to her far-removed brother. "You stood there and watched him die."

Lydia sat in the blood-soaked sand as anger, fear, and hate crawled their way into her soul.

CHAPTER 18

When her arms could no longer hold the body of her beloved, Lydia released Stephen into the hands of the six men who had faithfully served beside him over the last year.

Nicolaus reached over and closed Stephen's eyes.

Lydia watched the ginger color fade behind his olive eyelids. Her future seemed to close with them.

With great care, the men worked to remove Stephen's body from the pit and transport him back toward the city.

Lydia followed the slow march to Jerusalem. Her legs barely held the weight of her sorrow and grief. Even the stone steps, warmed by sunlight, sent chills through her sandals and up her body. She kept her eyes on Stephen as the men carried him through the streets toward the villa. Though the streets burst with life around her, her world had come to a sudden stop.

Inside the priest's home, the six men deposited the body to be properly prepared and shared the events that unfolded earlier in the day.

Lydia listened to broken conversations whirl around her as she sat next to Stephen.

Nicolaus informed James that it was Nicodemus who sought him out when Stephen was brought before the council. The member of the Sanhedrin and Way

Follower feared the outcome of the accusations and hurried to find Nicolaus. By the time they made it back to the Temple, the stoning had already begun.

He leaned closer to James and whispered more information into his ear.

Lydia heard her name, but nothing more of the private conversation.

The six men departed the villa with promises to spread the word of Stephen's death through the city and to return to assist with the burial.

When the room grew still, Lydia stared at Stephen. With his eyes now closed, he almost looked like he was sleeping. His expression held peace. Was he at peace?

Whispers and murmurs swirled around her. She didn't care to focus on any of the voices. Footsteps came and went for several moments until only she remained.

Lydia sat in the silent room. She watched Stephen's chest for any sign of movement. She recalled Martha's account of the last days she and her sister sat watch over Lazarus before he died. Her friend had shared that those were some of the most painful of her life.

The sound of footsteps caused Lydia to lift her head.

Her mother, followed by Salome, Elissa, and Arava, carried an assortment of spices, oils, and cloths into the room.

Each woman set down trays and bowls around Stephen and knelt to encircle him.

Mary put a gentle hand on Lydia's arm. "Would

you like to help?"

Lydia snatched her arm away from her mother's touch but didn't respond to her question.

Mary let out a sigh and signaled for the others to begin.

In the quiet, the women tenderly removed Stephen's torn tunic, washed his wounds, applied oils, rubbed in spices, and wrapped him like a newborn child.

Scents of myrrh and aloe mingled in the air around Lydia. The rich, earthy smells tickled her nose as she watched her family prepare the body of her betrothed.

After the others finished the last wrappings, Mary held up a cloth to Lydia.

She stared at the folded material.

"It's the one from Jesus' burial," Mary announced. "John retrieved it from the tomb the day they found it empty. He's been holding on to it." She rubbed the cloth between her fingers. "We agreed it best to let it lie with Stephen."

With trembling fingers, Lydia reached for the cloth. The soft material gave way in her hand. She held onto it for several heartbeats before laying it across Stephen's face. She placed a hand over the cloth, whispering a silent prayer and withdrew her arm.

Mary gently wrapped Stephen's head, covering the cloth.

With no other words, the women left, leaving Lydia alone once again with Stephen's body. A flash of bright ginger eyes filled her mind, causing her to bury her face in her hands and let out a loud wail. She'd never look into his eyes again.

She wasn't sure how long the others had been gone, but her tears were dried when her mother returned.

This time, Mary was alone when she entered. "I have this for you." She lowered herself beside Lydia and held out a dress.

Lydia stared at the awful sackcloth. She recognized it immediately. A widow's garment; her mother's widow garment. Mary wore the dark tunic for an entire year after the death of Joseph. Lydia remembered that dreadful year of mourning. Her skin itched at the memory of the sackcloth she wore for her father.

Even though she and Stephen had not yet celebrated their marriage feast, in the eyes of the law, they were as good as married. Her gaze was transfixed on the horrendous material. With it, she'd be marked as a widow before she got the chance to be a bride.

The grief of losing her father at such a young age collided with the sorrow over Stephen. Without the strength to stand, as tradition dictated, Lydia reached toward the right shoulder of her blue dress and tugged at the material until she heard the satisfying sound of tearing. She snatched the mourning garment from her mother's hands and shoved it over her head.

"Lydia—"

"You want me to wear it?" She yanked the dark dress into place over her blue one. "There."

Mary's gaze dropped to the floor. She slowly rose and left the room without another word.

Heat poured into Lydia's cheeks. The woven goat's

hair scratched at her neck and wrists. She could not bear the thought of parting with the blue dress Stephen gave her. If she was required to wear the dreadful garment, it would keep its place over her beloved's blue dress.

Lydia gazed over Stephen's wrapped body. Martha's plight of losing Lazarus came back to her. The sisters watched their brother lose his battle with the illness he fought all his life. Yet, after four days, Jesus recalled their brother from the grave. If only Jesus was here to call Stephen forth like he had for Lazarus. Fresh tears splashed on her face. "You watched him die and you're not even here to bring him back."

Salome entered the room, alone. She quietly made her way to Lydia and sat beside her. Without a word, she laid her head on Lydia's shoulder.

Lydia closed her eyes, allowing more tears to fall.

"His parents are here," Salome whispered. "Everyone's waiting." She lifted her head. "When you're ready."

Would she ever be ready?

Lydia knew exactly what the next steps would be. It must be close to sunset. She almost laughed at the thought that once again she was racing the setting sun. Only this time it was not chores she was trying to accomplish. This time she was holding back death's grip.

The men would come and carry Stephen's body to his family's tomb. They would place him inside and seal the door. Everyone would move on. She'd have to move on… without Stephen. Death would win. Saul had won. The viper had dealt a deadly blow. Without Jesus here, there was no hope of a resurrection.

She leaned over and touched her forehead to Stephen's. Whispering her devotion to him, she slowly rose. She would not stand in the way of custom. If Stephen could talk, he'd plead for his body to be at rest before the day's end. With only a few acts of honor available to give the man she loved, she turned and gave her sister a simple nod.

Salome retreated from the room and returned with the six men who'd served with Stephen. They moved his body onto a traveling bedroll and carried him out.

Lydia trailed them once more through the crowded streets. Unlike before, the mood of Jerusalem shifted. People stopped as they passed, crying out grief and sorrow. Tears fell. Heads bowed. Hands extended in comfort.

 Loud cries and wails echoed around her as she walked. Faces blurred in her vision as she fought to remain focused on Stephen. One of the benefits of being part of Abraham's family was that no Jew grieved alone.

Waiting at the gate were Stephen's parents, Amos and Orpah. The pair guided the processional out of the city walls to the place where their family lay.

At the entrance to the family's tomb stood five men, all ranging in different heights and builds, but they carried similar attributes that marked them as brothers.

Lydia searched the faces of each but didn't find the

unique eye color Stephen shared with his mother. Instead, their eyes were varying shades of their father's darker coloring.

She added her cries to the tumult as Stephen's body was laid among the bones of his ancestors. When the seal was placed to keep unwanted visitors out, she felt the weight of her new reality slammed into her. The burden of grief knocked her legs out from under her, and she hit the ground hard. Grabbing fists of dirt, she flung sand over her head and added more tears to the mix.

Her family, Stephen's, and her brother's followers all lifted their melodies of laments to the skies. The great commotion drew others to them.

Lydia noticed several widows approach the gathering. They were clothed in similar garments to hers. Though some wore more muted colors indicating the time of their mourning was ending.

She wondered how many of them could stand there because of Stephen's willingness to serve them. She listened to the sounds as their vocal despair combined with the others. With her betrothed entombed, she was now a widow with no Stephen to care for her.

CHAPTER 19

After the last cry of sorrow sounded and evening fell around them, the group dispersed back into the city.

Lydia retreated to the villa and retreated inward. For the next seven days, she'd sit shiva, mourning her lost betrothed. The tradition had become familiar to her while mourning her father, distant relatives, and most recently her oldest brother. She would be excused from all chores and social or cultural responsibilities for a week. It was a time to mourn, a time to reflect, a time to sit with sadness like an old friend.

Visitors of varying shapes and sizes filled the large house. They came from all corners of Jerusalem to mourn their shared loss. Many of those who had moved out of the villa stayed to weep and sit. During the day, they passed stories around like bread. Laughter mixed with tears.

Each moment shared was another stone heaped upon the pile of Lydia's shattered heart. By the third day, the villa felt like a prison. A cell of sorrow from which she believed she'd never escape. This time, death did not feel like an old friend. He felt like an enemy come to steal and destroy. To rob her of joy and hope. The longer she sat listening to stories of Stephen, the more her soul rotted.

With little expected of her and much forgiven,

Lydia often retreated to the outer courtyard to sit among her true friends. Boaz nuzzled her as if he knew her plight. The goats kept their vocalizations to a minimum. Even the chickens gave Lydia more space than normal. Elijah made frequent visits, bringing trinkets in exchange for her daily portions. A deal she happily made to see more of her feathered friend. What need did she have for food? What good would strength do a woman in mourning?

She sat among the piles of straw, fingering the edges of the blue garment under her sackcloth. Stephen's blood still stained the once beautiful dress. She noticed how the two colors mingled like the blue tassels of the priestly garments, often covered in the blood of sacrificed animals.

"Was that all he was to you?" she whispered to her brother, knowing Jesus could hear her even from his place in the clouds. "Was he simply an animal to be sacrificed on your altar?"

She watched Jacob and Esau play nearby. "You could have your pick of any number of animals, yet you chose Stephen."

A flash of a young boy's face with ginger eyes mocked her. "Among all this new life, you took Stephen. You took my one chance at life and left me with death." She shoved the dark sackcloth back over the blue dress.

After the week of mourning was complete, life in the villa returned to a normal routine for everyone except Lydia. She could hardly perform her chores and often wandered the house like a lost soul wandered the earth to which it didn't belong.

It was another week before she visited Naavah's home. The place she once found welcoming arms became a reminder of what she had lost. Even in the shadow cast by Stephen's death, Naavah and Joseph still planned to wed.

She regretted her decision to visit the moment she stepped into the home filled with women preparing for the upcoming marriage feast that should have been for her.

"Lydia," Naavah greeted her with soft kisses on both cheeks. "I'm glad to see you."

She clenched her jaw.

Naavah pulled her to one side of the room and spoke in a hushed tone, "I want you to know how truly sorrowful I am for your loss." She took a breath. "I know more than most what Stephen must have felt that day. When the crowd picked up rocks to stone me…" her voice trailed off. She shook her head. "It was one of the most terrifying moments of my life." She put her hand over her chest. "If it weren't for Jesus, I wouldn't be standing here. Your brother is the reason I've devoted my life to helping those removed from the Temple and their synagogues." She smiled. "I'm highly favored to join your family as well."

Lydia felt a guttural growl start in her midsection. *My brother spared you, an adulteress, while Stephen lies rotting on a slab.*

"Oh," Naavah said. "Speaking of brothers. I want to introduce you to my brother." She waved to a man across the room. "Reuben?"

The man excused himself and came toward them.

Naavah placed a hand on Lydia's arm. "Reuben, this is one of Joseph's sisters, Lydia."

"I'm sorry to hear of your recent loss." He dipped his head toward her. "A tragic event so close to a marriage feast."

Heat flamed Lydia's face. *What was supposed to be a double feast.*

"Lydia," Naavah patted her arm, "why don't you make yourself at home? I'll bring you something to eat." She set off toward the kitchen.

Lydia kept her eyes on Naavah's back. The last thing she wanted was food, but she wanted even less to be pitied. Without excusing herself from Reuben, she found an empty pillow near the wall and sat upon it.

Several moments later, Salome joined her side. "It's good to see you out of the villa." She pushed a plate of fruit toward Lydia. "I can't imagine the pain you must carry."

Lydia shook her head.

Salome lowered the offering. She was quiet for a long while before she spoke again. "I've overheard James and Jude talking about us."

Curious, Lydia raised her attention.

"They want to send us back to Nazareth," she admitted in a low voice. "They think we'll be safer there."

Lydia lifted an eyebrow at her sister.

"After Stephen's…" her voice trailed off. "After the stoning, there have been greater threats to Way Followers. It seems the council is prepared to stop us by force. Our growing numbers scare them. They want to stop us now before we grow beyond their reach."

Saul. His smirk danced in her vision. Heat rushed through her, and she jumped to her feet. Without a word to anyone, she stormed out of the house and into the small outer courtyard.

She huffed and screamed through gritted teeth, pacing the square. "That evil snake. This is all his fault."

"Kraa."

The familiar sound of Elijah's call grabbed her attention.

He hopped along the short stone wall of the courtyard.

Lydia stepped closer, noticing something shining in his beak. "What have you got there?" She held out her hand.

Elijah opened his mouth and deposited a small coin into her palm.

Holding up the piece of silver, she examined it. "Where did you get this?"

Elijah hopped up and down, squawking at her.

"Here." She pulled a handful of almonds from her tunic. "But we mustn't steal." She held the nuts out for him.

Accepting the trade, Elijah pecked the almonds from her hand and then flew away in a flutter of black wings.

Lydia turned the coin over and over in her fingers. "If Saul were out of the way, my family could live in Jerusalem without fear." She rubbed the face of Caesar etched into the coin. "I thought I finally figured out what Adonai had planned for me. Then Saul took everything."

Blood for blood. The voice which had spoken to her in the Temple returned with a haunting reminder.

She wrapped her fingers around the metal. "If Adonai requires blood for blood, why can't I?"

"Moses demanded it."

Rueben's voice caused her to jump.

"Forgive me." He bowed his head toward her. "I couldn't help overhearing." He took a step closer. "Didn't Moses say, 'If a man willfully attacks another to kill him by cunning, you shall take him from my altar, that he may die?'"

"Saul didn't lay a hand on Stephen."

"But are his hands not soaked in your betrothed's blood all the same?"

She couldn't deny that Saul approved of Stephen's murder.

"I know you don't know much about me." Reuben leaned against the half wall. "But I know people who can help you with your... problem."

Lydia searched his face, attempting to measure the truth among his words.

"People who would be glad to get rid of Saul as much as you." He rubbed his bearded chin. "If you're willing to pay the right price, that is."

She glanced down at the coin in her hand. "My brother was sold for thirty pieces of silver. Seems a fitting price for a life."

"You're in possession of such an amount?"

She closed her fingers around the coin and met his gaze. "My dowry."

Reuben nodded. "Bring it to me, and I will make the arrangements."

CHAPTER 20

In the next week, Lydia only ventured into the city once. It was a brief trip to deposit her dowry into Reuben's hands. She gladly exchanged the coins that were supposed to see her through a year of mourning for the promise of Saul's blood.

She spent much of her time in the outer courtyard to escape the preparations happening inside the villa.

Gray painted the sky, revealing a storm on the horizon.

Lydia sighed as she dragged herself back inside to avoid the rain.

The open areas of the villa bustled with activity. Women moved from space to space, cleaning, decorating, and cooking.

It was all supposed to be mine. Lydia watched her mother direct Jude to move a table closer to the wall. *Mine and Stephen's.*

Every flower and platter screamed the absence of her betrothed. She picked at a red anemone, remembering Stephen's excitement in meeting Lazarus during Jude's wedding feast. She inhaled the soft scent of the flower before crushing it into her palm and allowing the broken petals to fall to the floor.

The large front door swung open.

Lydia turned to find Benjamin standing in the

entryway.

"Naomi?" He rushed inside. "Has anyone seen Naomi?"

Mary hurried to him. "What's happened?"

"There's been a stabbing at the market."

Lydia couldn't help the smile that tugged at her lips. She imagined Saul bleeding from a dagger wound. Though she would have preferred a stoning for a stoning, as long as the injury resulted in his death it didn't matter. Justice would be dealt.

Benjamin searched the room. "They've called for a physician, but I thought Naomi could help." He made his way back to the door. "She wasn't at her house. I thought she might be here. Have you seen her?"

"Not today." Mary trailed behind him. "Who was stabbed?"

"I didn't see. I was in my booth when the shouts started," he admitted. "I've got to find Naomi." He went out the door without closing it behind him.

Lydia saw the open door. There had been nothing for her on the other side since the day they laid Stephen in his tomb. The city's siren song stopped calling to her. She took a step closer. The treasures of the market lost their allure. She took another step. The houses of friends stood as reminders of what she no longer had. She took another step. But now, somewhere in the market, Saul lay dying. She took the last step toward the door and placed her hand on the wood. The smell of coming rain danced in the air.

An ache rose in her to have the murderer of her beloved look upon her face as he took his final breath.

She quietly slipped out and headed toward the market.

The streets were busy with normal activity. As she passed through an archway, the sky opened, releasing a flow of water upon Lydia. She continued as rain soaked through her double layer of tunics.

In the center of the market street, people crowded around a spot, blocking her view of the injured.

She slipped through the throng to edge closer and closer. Twisting sideways, she pressed herself between two women, securing a place in the inner circle of witnesses.

Lydia's breath caught as she stared into the face of Saul.

He sat on the ground, clutching Penelope in his arms. Rain dripped from his dark hair and mixed with the blood spread across the top half of Penelope's tunic. He looked up and caught her gaze. His jaw hung open as he released a gut-wrenching wail.

Dropping her gaze to Penelope, Lydia's legs quaked under her dresses. The young woman's eyes were as empty as Stephen's had been. There was no doubt in her mind that she was already gone.

Naomi arrived and pushed past her. The midwife dropped to her knees to examine the girl. She pressed her ear against Penelope's mouth and then to her chest.

When she declared there was nothing more she could do, Saul let out another wail.

Unable to face the scene a second longer, Lydia fled back toward the villa. She hurried through the open space meticulously decorated for a wedding feast not her own and retreated to the outer courtyard.

Running past the animals, she flung herself on the damp straw under the overhang and wept. She screamed and moaned against the thunder that sounded around her.

Visions of Penelope's dark eyes clashed against Stephen's vacant stare. She beat her fists against the hay, screaming curses on Saul. Why had he approved of Stephen's death? Why did he hate Way Followers? She tore at her hair. Why had Penelope been caught between Saul and his just death sentence?

She buried her face in the straw and cried out, "Why have You let all this happen?"

The only sound she heard in response was the thunder as it echoed through the city.

Boaz's nuzzle startled her sometime later.

Lydia looked around to realize time had passed, but she was unsure how much. The rain had ceased, and the sky was growing darker. She picked hay from her hair and made her way inside the villa.

The house was quiet and still until a clang came from the kitchen.

She went to discover the source.

Alone in the room stood Salome, washing dishes.

Lydia approached her. "Sister?"

Salome slowly looked up. Her eyes were red and her cheeks held tear stains.

"What's happened?" Lydia looked around. "Where is everyone?"

Without an answer, Salome cleared the space between them and enveloped Lydia. "Everyone is looking for Simon."

"Simon?" Her wayward brother's name felt odd on her lips. She'd not heard his name mentioned in over a year. "Why would they be searching for Simon?"

Salome pulled back to look Lydia in the eyes. "James and Joseph are convinced he is the one who killed Penelope."

The red of Penelope's tunic and Stephen's marred skin competed for her vision. She shook them away. "Why would they think that?"

Releasing her hold on Lydia, Salome grabbed her braid and twisted the ends in her fingers. "Some witnesses claim to have seen a man in a gray tunic near Penelope before she collapsed." She shoved her hair over her shoulder. "From the descriptions, James and Joseph think it's Simon. They're trying to find him before the council or the Romans find him first."

"What are they going to do with him if they find him?"

"I don't know." Salome shrugged. "But I shudder to think what Rome will do if they find him before our brothers do. Penelope's family is well-known to Caesar's household."

A tremor ran up Lydia's back. Would she lose another brother to Rome's hand?

"James knew Pilate would send out as many troops as he could spare," Salome continued. "After what happened with Jesus, I'm sure he's not eager for a report of the murder of a respected Roman's daughter to make its way to Caesar's court."

"Do you think they'll find Simon?"

Salome's eyes grew large. "I hope so."

Several hours later, the rest of the family returned to the villa without Simon.

Lydia pulled James aside. "Did you find any trace of him?"

"None." James hung his head. "It's as if he's a spirit."

"What if it wasn't him?"

James searched her face. "According to the witnesses, it has to be."

"But what if it's not?" She twisted her hands together. "What if it were someone else?"

"Someone who looks like our brother, wearing a gray cloak, carrying a dagger, and stabbing people?" James' words dripped with cynicism. "We already know he's capable of such. You remember what he did to Joseph?"

"But Simon was careful," Lydia argued. "He knew exactly where to place his blade, so he didn't kill Joseph."

James sighed. "We haven't seen Simon in over a year. Maybe he stopped being careful."

"What if it were someone else?" Lydia pleaded.

James lifted a brow at her. "Do you know something you're not sharing?"

She shook her head. "I just don't think Simon would intentionally murder anyone."

"If it wasn't him," James eased, "we still need to find him. For his own good." He looked toward the others. "We need to pull him out of whatever mess he's gotten himself into." He walked away, carrying the weight of the situation on his drooping shoulders.

Lydia's insides twisted. Was Simon involved with Reuben? How had Penelope ended up on the wrong end of the blade instead of Saul? There were so many unanswered questions that tugged at her soul.

CHAPTER 21

Joseph and Naavah's wedding feast arrived with great joy for everyone except Lydia. She spent the day hiding among the animals, refusing to take part in the final preparations.

As evening drew near, Mary marched into the outer courtyard, hands on her broad hips. "Lydia bat Joseph, you get yourself in this house at once."

Lydia lay on her side among the hay.

"I'm not going to repeat myself." Mary folded her arms across her chest. "This is an important night for your brother."

Lydia twirled a loose blade of grass between her fingers, taking notice of her torn fingernails.

"I know the pain you carry is great." Mary took a step closer and lowered her tone. "No one wanted this more for you than I." She let out a weighted sigh. "No one can bring Stephen back, but it would mean everything for you to be part of Joseph's celebration." She let her request hang in the air for several moments before she turned and went back inside.

"You could." Lydia didn't lift her head to address her sky-dwelling brother. "You raised Lazarus, and Jairus' daughter, and a widow's son. Even yourself, Hiram, and others all walked out of your tombs." She huffed. "Why not Stephen?" She turned to recline on her back. "You waited four days to call Lazarus from his tomb. Is a month too long?"

The fading light cast long shadows over her. Rhythmic breathing from sleeping animals surrounded her.

"Tonight was to be the night Stephen and I were to join as one." She sighed. "After a long year of waiting, I was to have all I ever wanted. What do I have now?"

She instinctively lifted her sackcloth to reveal the bottom of her stained blue dress and methodically fingered the material. "I have nothing now," she answered her own question, knowing Jesus wasn't going to answer her.

Footsteps echoed in the courtyard.

Lydia shifted to see who was coming, half expecting her mother to return to drag her inside. Instead, she saw a pair of men's sandals approach.

"Lydia?"

She recognized the voice of Nicolaus and rose, adjusting her sackcloth back over her blue dress.

"There you are." He halted. "Your mother said you were out here."

She dipped her head to one side.

Nicolaus gazed around her. "Stephen said you enjoy spending time with animals."

The mention of her beloved's name was a dagger to her heart.

"I didn't mean to upset you." Nicolaus took a small step closer. "Stephen was like a brother to me." He pressed his palm over his chest. "We spent months together caring for the widows. It gave us many opportunities to talk."

The tightness in Lydia's chest eased slightly.

"He spoke a lot about you." One side of Nicolaus' mouth turned upward. "He was looking forward to this night."

As was I. She attempted to storm past him, but he blocked her way. She squinted at him.

"I can't imagine what you must be thinking and feeling right now. Believe me," he let out a single chuckle, "I would give anything not to share with you what's on my mind."

"Then keep it behind your lips." She tried to move around him a second time.

"I would." He darted between her and the door. "If I could."

She stomped her foot. "What is so pressing that you must seek a woman in mourning and prevent her from attending her brother's wedding feast?"

Nicolaus rubbed the back of his neck with one hand and lifted the other in helplessness. "Stephen asked me to do something in case anything ever happened to him."

"What?"

"Take you as my bride."

His words hit her like stones, weighing her down and breaking through her carefully constructed defense. "I beg your pardon?"

"Every time we left the home of a poor widow, Stephen would talk." Nicolaus dropped his hands. "He would talk about you and how it would crush him if you were ever put into a position like them. He cared so much for you that he never wanted you to live in need."

The tenderness of Stephen collided with the absurdity of the man's claims. "I don't even know you."

"I know." Nicolaus laughed. "But Stephen did. We shared much of our lives in the last year. Lydia, believe me, I wouldn't dare approach you about this if I were not honor-bound to Stephen." He ventured a step toward her. "He made me promise you would not live as a helpless widow. That I must do everything in my power to see you cared for... as he would have done."

The internal ache became too much for Lydia to bear. "Leave me alone," she seethed. "Why can't everyone just leave me alone?" She pushed past him and stormed inside.

Sounds of music and laughter filled the villa. The flicker of oil lamps cast dancing shadows on the walls. Joy slammed into her sorrow like a hammer on stone, causing greater cracks in her already fractured soul. Tears burned her eyes.

"Greetings."

Lydia froze. She thought the voice belonged to Nicolaus, whom she guessed followed her inside. She turned to stare into the face of Naavah's brother, Reuben.

He leaned against a wall, swirling a cup in one hand, and resting his other hand on his leather belt. "I've been searching for you all night."

Lydia glanced around.

Reuben pressed off the wall and came closer to her.

"I'm sure by now you've heard the good news."

Penelope's vacant stare flashed in her vision.

"Your little problem having been dealt with?"

The vile stench of too much wine breathed on Lydia, mixing with his words. "It wasn't supposed to be her." She looked around again, making sure no one was close enough to hear their conversation. "It was supposed to be him."

"She was the better target." He took a sip from his cup.

"I never meant for her to get hurt." She swallowed hard. "I wanted *him* gone."

Reuben lifted a shoulder and emptied his cup. "Regardless, it seems your funds were only enough for a deposit."

"Deposit?"

"Yes, though the job was complete," he tilted the cup to his lips again, frowning at the empty vessel, "it seems my connection desires the rest of his payment."

"The rest?" She shook her head. "I gave you all I have."

"That's too bad." He slowly lowered the cup. "But I'm sure you have plenty of ways of getting the rest." He circled her, looking around the room. "This sure is a pleasant villa. The owner must be doing well."

Lydia's mind went to Theodotus and all he provided for her family. Minor quakes went through her. "I have no direct access to the priest's funds."

"No?" He clicked his tongue. "Shame." He continued slowly circling her. "Naavah also tells me there are lots of people who give your family money."

"Those funds go directly to helping widows survive." She straightened her back to stop her trembling. "Those coins do not pass through my hands."

Reuben hesitated in front of her. "And how would your dear family feel if they learned you hired someone to spill blood for you?"

A shiver ran down her back, weakening her knees. "You wouldn't."

He turned his face toward the crowd and opened his mouth.

"Enough." She held up her hands. "I yield. How much?"

"Another thirty pieces."

"T-thirty?" The amount caught in her throat. "How am I supposed to get that much?"

Reuben let his gaze drift downward. "I'm sure you'll come up with something." His eyes returned to her face. "If not, I'll tell the council what you did."

A familiar set of broad shoulders squeezed between Lydia and Reuben. "Don't think we've had the pleasure of meeting."

Lydia's fingers flew to her lips in recognition of someone she'd not laid eyes on in months. "Hiram?"

He flicked a curious glance over his shoulder at her before returning his attention to Reuben.

Lydia glanced around him to see Reuben's neck shifting to red. "Don't think your guard here is going to keep me away." He set a stern glare on her. "I know your secret, and if you intend to keep it that way, you'll do as I ask."

She nodded slowly.

Reuben turned on his heel, leaving Hiram with a piercing stare, and disappeared into the celebration.

Lydia felt her entire body whither.

Hiram turned to face her directly. "Who was that?"

She took a steadying breath. "Naavah's brother, Reuben."

"Seemed like a pretty tense conversation."

She nodded.

"Something you'd like to share?"

Tears pushed forward. "Hiram, I think I'm in trouble."

CHAPTER 22

Lydia watched Hiram's left eyebrow slowly raise.

"What kind of trouble?"

"The worst kind."

Hiram looked around. "Anywhere we can talk?"

Lydia noticed the kitchen was nearby. She waved toward the area.

With only a sliding glance toward the large room, he shook his head. "Not there."

"Come." She led him through the house to a back storage room. "I don't think anyone will interrupt us in here."

The chamber was lined with shelves stacked with supplies, and vessels of all shapes and sizes filled the space thanks to the gracious funds of people and priests.

Lydia lit a small oil lamp and set it on a shelf near some oil jars. The chill in the vacant room caused her to pull her headscarf closer around her neck. "I haven't seen you in months," she tried an easier topic, not yet ready to divulge her plight. "Where have you been?"

Hiram plucked a small bottle of perfume off a shelf and held it up to his nose. "All over Judea." He returned the container to its place. "I was quite angry with James for taking in that Roman soldier." He laid his hand on the shelf. "I had come to the villa that day to discuss marrying Salome. But when I saw the Roman, I lost my temper." He pounded his fist on the shelf, causing the items upon it to rattle.

Lydia jumped at the sound.

"Sorry." He turned away from the wall. "That Roman almost killed Salome. I couldn't bear to lose another woman I cared about to the hands of Rome."

Lydia watched the lamp light dance on his face, illuminating several faint scars. Her youngest sister's smile leapt to mind. She wondered if the girl was aware of Hiram's intentions. Lydia knew Assia had suspicions about the two, but Hiram was not the most open of individuals.

"So, I ran away," he admitted. "I've been traveling from city to city looking for a fresh start. And you know what I found? Nothing." He shook his head. "There were no answers out there. In every new place I tried to settle, I still woke up the same person. The same man carrying the same weight of hatred in my soul."

He paced around the small area. "It wasn't until I figured out that I had to lay everything down that I finally saw the truth. My problem wasn't with the Romans, it was with me. I had to let Adonai deal with me. I only just arrived back in Jerusalem when I heard about Stephen." He glanced in her direction.

Lydia clenched her jaw.

"Stephen was a fine man. One of the best I've ever known. I came to grieve him along with the others." He let his fingertips trail the edge of another shelf. "James cornered me afterward and asked where I'd been. I shared about what Adonai was doing with me, and we had a long talk. I'm still not sure what the future holds for me, but I know I can't keep letting my past direct my steps. That's Adonai's job."

She wanted to argue, but she, too, was in a war with her past. Her choices led to fatal mistakes and her next steps were uncertain. "Hiram?"

He stopped.

"I killed someone."

"You what?" He closed the gap between them.

"It wasn't my hand," she raised her hand, imagining blood soaking her fingertips, "but the blame is on me all the same."

"Lydia, you're not making sense."

She closed her fingers as if gripping the handle of a dagger and plunged the unseen weapon into her midsection. Hot tears burned her eyes. "Penelope, Saul's betrothed. It's my fault she's dead."

"Tell me everything."

With tears pouring down her face, Lydia recounted the entire story. How Saul treated her in the market, his veiled threats the day she visited the synagogue of the Freedman, her betrothal to Stephen, and the day Stephen taught in the synagogue resulting in the stoning. She shared her weeks of mourning and the single thought of revenge for Saul taking her beloved.

"I wanted him dead," she openly admitted. "With a smile on his lips, he killed the only man I've ever loved." Her insides turned at the memory of Saul's smug face. "He didn't deserve to keep breathing while Stephen lay decaying in a tomb."

She sniffled. "Naavah's brother said he could help. Said if I paid him, he had people who also wanted Saul gone and he could make it happen."

"But how did Penelope end up dead?"

"I don't know." She shook her head. "When I confronted Reuben about that, he said she was the better target. I didn't understand what he meant."

"Sending a message to Rome." Hiram pinched the place between his eyes. "It's what I would have done in my former life."

"That's not the worst part."

"What is?"

Lydia sighed. "James thinks Simon is the one who held the blade."

"Did anyone see him?"

"The witnesses were unsure." She lifted a shoulder. "But from all accounts, James is convinced. He's spent days searching for him."

"If Simon truly struck the blow, he'd be deep in hiding at this point. James will never find him."

"What do I do?"

"I know someone who can help." Hiram let his head hang low. "Someone who helped me when I was in trouble. You need to speak with Rabbi Ethan. He'll know what to do."

"Can he really help?"

"He's helped many." He moved toward the door. "But we'll have to go to him."

"Didn't he perform the ceremony this evening?"

"He did." Hiram glanced over his shoulder. "But he left soon after with a promise to return tomorrow."

"I don't think Reuben is going to give me much mercy."

"I don't either." He reached over to extinguish the lamp. "We need to go to Rabbi Ethan tonight."

Lydia led Hiram out of the back of the house and into the streets of the Upper City.

Hiram took the lead from there, marching through the shadows toward the synagogue the older rabbi called home.

After several loud pounds on the wooden door, Rabbi Ethan appeared disheveled and clearly roused from a deep sleep. "Hiram?"

Hiram stepped aside, revealing Lydia.

The Rabbi pulled his tunic into a proper place. "Has something happened?"

"May we come in?" Hiram pushed his way in without waiting to be invited.

Lydia followed, keeping her head down.

Ethan shut the door behind her and moved to light a few oil lamps. As he did, their glow washed through the empty synagogue.

The stone steps shone bright in the dim flickers.

Lydia sat down on a bottom slab and set her face in her hands. "I've done something terrible, Rabbi." Between her sobs, she once more shared her woes with Saul and her deal with Reuben.

When she was finished, Ethan took the seat next to her and folded his arms across his body. "Does your family know?"

"No." Lydia put her hands on his arm. "They can't know what I've done."

"I think you need to tell them."

"They'll never understand."

"Oh, I don't know about that."

Lydia wiped at her damp face. "If I tell them what I've done, they'll never forgive me."

"I'm not certain of that either." Ethan eased back. "In fact, they might be the people who forgive you the fastest."

"What do you mean?"

"Look at Joseph." Ethan patted the tops of her hands. "He has forgiven Naavah of her past choices, and they are united as one."

"Naavah didn't have anyone murdered." Lydia huffed.

"True." He squeezed her fingers. "But she sinned against her former husband and against Adonai."

Lydia considered how difficult it must have been for Joseph to look past the reputation of an adulteress to see a bride.

"Love is a choice, Lydia. So is forgiveness." Ethan smiled behind his thick, gray beard. "The difference is that forgiveness has a lot less to do with the other person and much more to do with one's relationship with Adonai."

"How so?"

"Consider your brother Jesus."

"Jesus?"

"Yes." He gestured in the air. "The man who deserved a death sentence the least of any who's stepped foot on the ground, and yet He didn't withhold forgiveness to those who took His life. He asked Adonai to forgive them."

Lord, do not hold this sin against them. The last words of Stephen rang through her. "Stephen did too."

"Because of their relationship with Adonai."

"Wasn't it Moses who said, 'But if there is harm, then you shall pay life for life, eye for eye, tooth for tooth, hand for hand, foot for foot, burn for burn, wound for wound, stripe for stripe'?"

"Obeying that law would leave us all blind and dead." He looked deep into her eyes. "You can't find your life by only following the letter of the law. Believe an old rabbi. You must discover who you are in your relationship with Adonai."

"What do I do?"

"Be cleansed, confess what you've done, and ask for forgiveness."

"Reuben doesn't want words, he wants coins. If I don't pay him, he's going to turn me into the council." She shook her head. "He wants another thirty pieces. I gave him my entire dowry. I don't have anything else to give."

Ethan rose and moved toward the back of the synagogue.

Lydia looked to Hiram, who had made himself comfortable across the room.

He stretched and rose to draw near her.

"Do you really think it'll be that simple?" She rose from her place.

"Oh, it's not going to be simple, but that doesn't make it unnecessary."

Ethan returned. "Take this." He extended a money

pouch in her direction. "This should buy his silence."

"I can't accept that." Lydia took a step back. "I'll never be able to pay it back."

"None of us can ever pay the sin debts we owe." He shook the pouch. "That doesn't stop Adonai from paying it on our behalf."

"I'll make sure Reuben gets this." Hiram accepted the pouch and tucked it into his leather belt. "Along with a clear message." He marched out of the synagogue.

"Thank you." She kissed Ethan's cheek and followed Hiram out.

CHAPTER 23

After a fitful night, Lydia woke to the light of a new day. *I know what I need to do, Lord. Help me do it.*

It had been too late when she returned from Rabbi Ethan's last night to speak with her family. She elected instead to get a good night's sleep and be ready to face her next steps with the dawn. Though dawn had come, she'd not gotten much rest. Dreams haunted her. Still, she needed to face what lay ahead.

She quietly rolled up her sleeping mat before moving toward the doorway.

Salome stirred. "Where are you going so early?" her voice held the sound of a yawn.

"I'm taking back what my enemy has stolen from me." Lydia marched out of the room and down the stairs toward the inner courtyard.

First, she'd take back her relationship with Adonai, then her family, and finally her future. She wasn't sure how she'd regain the latter two, but she had a good idea of how to cleanse her soul before her Lord.

East of the courtyard, Lydia took a set of broad steps down to the lower level of the house. Most of the rooms on the level were used for storage, but one had been paved with black and white stones, forming a beautiful mosaic. The plastered room with a vaulted ceiling housed a large water collection, which was used by the priest's household as a mikvah.

Taking each step slowly, Lydia noted the extravagant room. In comparison, the mikvah in Nazareth paled to all the ones in Jerusalem. The small underground room was plainly plastered and filled with rainwater in the rainy season and with water from the cisterns in hotter months. She visited the pool every month since she was a young girl, cleansing her body from her ritual uncleanness.

She'd done the same every month since moving to Jerusalem. Though the grandeur of the priest's mikvah made the time feel more special.

Near the steps leading down into the water, fresh cloths lay waiting for those who needed to cleanse themselves. She took one and descended the last steps.

Shivers ran up her legs as her toes made contact with the cooler stones. Waiting at the last step before the water, she hesitated. It was not the time to cleanse herself of her physical impurity, but she needed to cleanse her soul from her spiritual impurity.

She deposited the cleansing cloth on the step above her and lifted the dark sackcloth dress first. Once free of the awful material, she dropped it on the same step.

The blue dress stained with Stephen's blood reflected the blue of the water. She stared down at the spots that had darkened over the long month since the stoning. With care, she lifted the dress over her head and held it in her hands. She ran her fingers over each mark, recounting every memory of her beloved. The first time they met. The sound of his laughter. The way his ginger eyes gazed into her soul.

Folding the garment, she set it next to the sackcloth. The pair of dresses filled the step, reflecting her last few weeks. Joy and sorrow sitting side by side. Happiness had overcome her as the days of the wedding feast drew near. Then she was plunged into the depths of grief after losing Stephen.

She removed her linen undergarment and laid it on top of the pile.

Turning to face the waters, she noticed her vague reflection staring back at her. The still waters created an effect similar to her polished bronze. Dipping her toe into the water disturbed the reflection. Her foot found the next step and the next until she was submerged in the water.

Past the steps, she swam toward the center of the small pool. The cool water felt refreshing on her dry skin. She'd not cared for herself since the stoning and could only imagine the stench that had accumulated along with the dirt.

She took in a deep breath, closed her eyes, and plunged herself beneath the water.

Silence engulfed her as water filled her ears. The sound of Stephen's voice echoed in her mind. *Lydia, nothing would bring me greater honor than for you to be my bride.*

She smiled to herself as his ginger eyes flashed in her memory. *I miss you, beloved.*

Her lungs burned, causing her to resurface. Breaking through the water, she remembered taking her turn in the pool of Siloam on the day of the fiery tongues. Her swim in the mikvah was like a second bath in the warm fire of Adonai's presence.

The cool water washed away the filth from her outsides while the fire of Adonai burned away the mire that clung to her soul. Tears pooled in her eyes. How had she allowed hate to blemish her soul?

Paddling back toward the steps, she considered her next task. *James.* The mere thought of her brother's name sent a shiver of dread through her as she found the bottom step. She would need to seek her patriarch and tell him the truth. Would he listen? Would he turn her over to the council himself?

With each step out of the water, she felt her conviction firm. No matter what the result would be, she needed to confess her wrongs and leave the results in Adonai's hands.

Emerging from the pool, she stood on the last dry step and stared down at her garments. Taking the cleaning cloth, she dried herself as best she could manage and then slipped her under linen over her clean skin. She wanted nothing more than to cover it with the beautiful blue dress that had only known her body. Yet, she still had several months before she could exchange sackcloth for bright colors once more.

Her gaze shifted to the scratchy material. The dress was uncomfortable on purpose. Mourning wasn't intended to be a pleasing season. She'd still need to endure the fabric until she properly mourned Stephen, but at least she could release the blue dress. For now.

She picked up the dark sackcloth and lifted it over her head, adjusting it into place.

Collecting her blue dress and the cleaning cloth,

she ascended the stairs to the courtyard. She deposited the cloth where it would be added to others of its kind for washing. She held onto the stained dress and considered her options. Burning the dress would not be beyond reason. It was ruined; the stains having sat for weeks. She couldn't bring herself to even entertain the idea. It was a gift from Stephen. She sighed. Perhaps her mother would know the best course for ridding the garment of its stains. The dip in the mikvah had cleansed her body and soul. It wouldn't be enough for the dress.

She tucked the garment among her small pile of belongings and sought her brother.

James was gathered with many of the others in the upper room.

Lydia entered to discover food had been laid out for them, but none of it touched. The room was filled with hushed conversations, and the air felt thick with fear.

She searched the men's faces, knowing she wouldn't find Stephen among them, but several others were missing as well. She went to James. "Where are Timon and Prochoru?"

"Arrested."

The simple word sent a tremor through her. "What?"

"Along with Andronicus."

Her fingers flew to her lips. "Junia?"

"Safe, as far as we know."

"What happened?"

James looked into her eyes for a long moment

before he let out a heavy breath. "It's Saul."

The very name made her insides tremble. "He had his own uncle arrested?"

"He's on a mission. He's been storming houses and dragging off men and women accused of being Way Followers."

"How can he do that?"

James glanced around at the others. "He's got the approval of the council." He let his gaze come back to her. "I think he's searching for Simon."

"What are we going to do? We can't let him do this."

"There isn't anything we can do." James stepped toward her. "It's not safe here anymore." He took another steadying breath. "I've spoken with Joseph and Jude. We've agreed to send you and Salome back to Nazareth."

"Nazareth?" She shook her head. "I can't go back there."

CHAPTER 24

"Lydia, are you listening to me?" James raised his voice. "Saul is seeking all Way Followers. If he gets to us, he won't hesitate to fit you with chains alongside the rest of us. I can't let that happen."

Lydia's thoughts returned to her beloved. "But Stephen is buried here."

"You belong in Nazareth."

"I belong with Stephen."

"Stephen is with Jesus now."

She stomped her foot. "Then maybe I shall go to them both."

"Lydia, you will do as I say. I'm responsible for you."

She stared at her brother. His resolve was clearly etched into the deep lines on his face. What made her think James would understand? She couldn't tell him. Not now. She couldn't tell any of them what she'd done. He was going to send her away. Away from Stephen.

She couldn't take it. Turning on her heels, she fled the room and the villa. There was only one place she wanted to be; with her beloved.

Lydia ran through the streets of Jerusalem, out of the gate, and made her way toward the tomb of Stephen. She slowed as she approached. Her body objected to the sudden sprint with burning muscles. She placed her hand on the stone that separated her from the body of her beloved.

"Oh, Stephen. Why did you go that day to the synagogue?" She laid her forehead on the rock. "Why did you have to leave me?"

Her insides quaked. "James is trying to send me back to Nazareth. There is nothing for me in Nazareth." She slid to her knees. "You're here."

She rocked her head back and forth against the stone. "It's my fault Penelope is dead, and now Saul is hunting us. He wants more blood, as if yours wasn't enough. I don't think he's going to stop until we're all dead or in chains."

"Maybe I should turn myself over to him." She traced lines on the rock. "Though I don't know if I would be enough to sway his hunger. I don't think I will be enough to stop him."

A soft breeze fluttered her hair.

"Stephen, I want to be with you." She closed her eyes. "If my choices are a prison cell or a tomb, I'd rather lie next to you."

Memories flashed in her mind of the stones hurled at Stephen. "Maybe I should walk into the Temple and declare Jesus as Messiah so they would have no choice but to stone me, too." She took a breath. "Did it hurt, my love?" She retraced the lines of the stone. "At least your pain only lasted a little while. I've been dying every day without you, and the pain is getting too much to bear."

The next breeze carried a strange sound.

Lydia opened her eyes and looked around. "What was that?"

The echo of an awful noise sounded again.

"It sounds like an animal." She rose and leaned toward the sound. "Like an animal caught in a trap."

The sound grew until Lydia sought the distressed creature.

Near the tombs, over a set of jagged rocks, she noticed movement. She glanced around before approaching, but couldn't find another person in sight.

Drawing closer to the rocks, she discovered a tiny, naked infant. "A baby!" She moved closer to examine the babe.

Pale skin and streaks of fresh blood revealed the boy had been born recently and been exposed to the open air for much of the time.

"Who would leave a…" Junia's explanation of Roman rock children came back to her, answering her question before she could finish. The woman had adopted Shamira after finding the girl among the rocks. "Could this be a rock child?"

The babe wiggled and screamed.

Lydia's thoughts went to Joshua and Hadassah. Her aunt arms ached to calm the child. She tore off her headscarf and reached to wrap the young one with it.

"How could anyone simply abandon a child like this?" She wrapped him tight and held him close, attempting to warm him with her body.

As the boy's cries quieted, he opened his eyes. A flash of ginger stared up at her.

"Oh, my!" She held the boy toward the light, fully

convinced her own eyes were lying to her. Among a set of dark eyes, a glint of ginger flashed again. "Stephen?"

The boy continued his former protest.

"Forgive me." She pressed him against her chest once more. "You remind me of someone."

When the boy settled again, she stared into his unusual eyes. A gold color rimmed the dark coloring. They reflected a lostness she felt in her bones. "You've lost someone." She rocked him gently. "I have as well."

She bounced and paced in a circle. "What am I to do with you?"

"We'll be happy to dispose of that refuse for you."

Lydia froze, cradling the boy against herself. She looked up to see several men circling her. Many of them appeared to need a good bathing. "What do you want?"

The largest one stepped forward and pointed to her bundle. "We've come for that."

"You can't have him." She dug her fingers into the baby, causing him to cry out.

"Oh, but we can." He came nearer.

Lydia searched the face of each man, hoping to find one to reason with. When her eyes fell on the last man, she yelped, "Simon?"

The man in a dirty gray cloak straightened his back, revealing his full height.

"Simon, it's me," she pleaded.

Simon didn't respond.

The leader pressed himself closer to her. "Give us that child, and we'll let you go."

"I will not." Lydia took a step back, trying to put

space between herself and the large man while moving closer to Simon.

"Then we'll have to take him." He nodded toward Simon.

Reaching out, Simon grabbed for the boy.

"No!" Lydia yelled, moving the baby out of his grasp. "Simon, listen to me."

Simon made another attempt, but missed.

"Please don't do this," Lydia pleaded.

"Just give him what he wants," Simon growled.

"I can't do that." Lydia clung to the boy. "This is wrong. You know this is wrong."

"Enough!" the leader shouted. He swung his arm, knocking the baby from Lydia's hands and catching her arm in the process.

The boy let out a terrible wail as he hit the ground.

Pain shot up Lydia's arm. She ignored the agony and scrambled to regain possession of the boy.

The leader snatched the boy's leg before Lydia could reach him. He untangled the boy from the cloth, exposing his naked form once more, and held him up.

The baby's cry grew louder.

"Don't hurt him!" Lydia sobbed. "Please don't hurt him."

He removed his dagger from his belt and held the blade to the boy's throat. "Let his fate be the fate of every Roman."

"No!" Lydia lunged at the large man, swiping at the blade. Cold metal sliced through her hand, but she clung to it until she managed to knock the weapon from his grip. "Release him!" she screamed and dug her broken fingernails into the man's flesh.

He dropped the boy and used both hands to tear Lydia from himself. "You're mad, woman!" He shoved her to the ground.

Lydia thudded hard against the dirt. The pain in her arm screamed, and her vision went dark for a moment.

"Simon, take care of this mess." The leader turned away with his hand on his face.

The others followed.

Rising to fight again, Lydia's world twisted sideways. She reached for the sound of the baby's cries. "I won't let them hurt you." She rose on shaking legs. "I won't let them kill you, too."

Through blurred vision, she saw Simon kneel and reach for the baby. His dagger was already in hand as he scooped the baby into his open hand.

"No!" She lashed at him, but missed.

"Stop." He pointed the dagger toward her.

The glint of metal and the fire in his eyes caused her to hesitate.

Simon put the edge of the dagger to the baby's thigh.

"Simon, don't." Fresh tears blurred her vision and she reached for the boy.

He swiped his blade against the babe's flesh and dropped him.

The boy screamed.

"Simon, how could you?"

He rose and fled with his cloak flowing behind him.

Lydia threw herself onto the boy. Red stained her vision. "Not another one." She turned her face to the sky. "You're not taking any more from me."

She cradled the boy against her chest. "I won't let you have another one."

She retrieved her headscarf and pressed it against the baby's wound. There was only one place she could think of to take the boy. She looked toward the walls of Jerusalem and ran straight toward them.

Her feet flew through the city as she hoped she would find the midwife at home.

CHAPTER 25

"Naomi!" Lydia yelled, approaching the midwife's home. "Naomi!"

"Lydia?" Naomi rushed from her dwelling to meet her in the small courtyard. "What has—What is that?"

"Help." Lydia hurried past her into the house. "Please, you've got to help him."

Naomi followed her inside and reached out for the baby. "Give him to me."

Lydia extended her shaking arms.

"You're covered in blood." She flicked her chin to a nearby water jug. "Wash up and get me some cloths." She moved to set the boy on her low table. "Whose child is this?" She flung around. "Lydia, did you and Stephen…"

"He's not mine." Lydia scrubbed blood from her fingers, but the cut on her hand continued to bleed. "I found him near Stephen's tomb." She grabbed a stack of cloths, wrapped one around her injured hand, and laid the rest on the table next to the boy.

"A rock child?" Naomi whispered.

"That was my guess."

"Lydia, he's badly injured."

"Can you help him?"

Naomi snatched a cloth and wiped at the boy. "He's only hours old." She pointed to the mangled cord of flesh hanging from his midsection.

"Stephen would have been able to heal him." Lydia hung her head. "Like he did for Shamira."

"I'm only a midwife," she reminded her. "My herbs and mixtures can only do so much. Stephen had the power of Adonai flowing through his hands."

A large tear rolled down her cheek. "You've got to try."

Naomi gave a simple nod. "At least he's still breathing." She looked over her shoulder. "Hand me my bag. I've got to address these injuries."

Lydia fetched the sack and emptied the contents onto the table.

The boy let out a cry at the commotion.

Naomi cleared away the drying blood while examining the boy from head to toe. "I've heard of the arrests."

Lydia froze.

"It's a shame what the council is allowing." She clicked her tongue. "I pray this madness ceases soon or we may have an all-out war in this city."

Lydia watched Naomi's skilled hands while attempting to keep her thoughts off Saul and his hunt. She looked down into the helpless face of the little boy. "I don't understand how someone can throw away a child."

"People can find a thousand reasons to dispose of a child." Naomi looked up at her. "You only need one to keep them; love." She set to tending the open wound on the boy's thigh. "Are you going to tell me what happened here?"

"What do you mean?"

She gestured to the injury. "I've treated enough dagger wounds to know one when I see it."

Lydia flinched. "It was Simon."

"Your brother did this?"

"I don't know if my brother is still in the man who did this. The Simon I knew would never draw a weapon on a child." She sniffled. "He's entangled himself with some rough men."

"They wanted the boy dead, didn't they?"

"How did you know?"

Naomi sighed. "Not the first time I've experienced that either." She mixed some herbs, releasing their scents into the air. "By his features and complexion, he's clearly Roman. I suppose killing helpless babies is easier than taking on full-grown soldiers." She slathered the mix over the clean wound. "Cowards."

"But why not simply leave the rock children to the elements?"

"That used to be good enough." Naomi placed a cloth over the mix and wrapped the boy's leg. "Until Way Followers started rescuing them and raising them as their own."

"I know Junia found little Shamira on the rocks. You're saying there have been others?"

She nodded. "Many people have been taking your brother's teachings to heart. But others don't approve of such acts of mercy. You're favored to have been able to rescue him."

Lydia reached up to her head.

"And by the looks of it, you did so with a fight."

"I wasn't going to let them hurt Stephen."

"Stephen?"

Lydia tucked her head. "His eyes remind me of Stephen's."

Naomi took a large piece of material and fashioned a wrap to quiet his protests. "There. Now," she turned to Lydia, "let me have a look at you."

She brushed away her concerns. "I'll be fine."

"Your injuries say otherwise." She reached for her again. "Let me have some peace in examining you."

She submitted to Naomi's touch. "How bad is he?"

Naomie continued without answering.

She reached up to grab the midwife's arm. "How bad?"

"I can't be sure," Naomi admitted. "Most of his injuries are minor scrapes and bruises. The dagger wound is deep, possibly cut some muscles and tendons. He might have trouble with that leg."

Lydia released her hold. "We can live with that."

"You're serious." She dabbed at a cut on her head. "You want to raise this boy on your own? As a widow."

The truth stung. "I'll manage."

"And what about your family? How do you think they'll feel about all this?"

Lydia honestly didn't know. "I have a lot to discuss with them."

"I'll give you something for the ache." She moved toward a shelf.

Lydia pressed her fingers against her temple. "How did you know?"

"You'll have a nasty bump for a while." She handed

her a jar of willow tree bark. "But the swelling will go down. Now let me take a look at your hand."

Lydia held out her wrapped hand.

Naomi untied the loose bandage, examined the cut, and re-wrapped it with a clean cloth. "We'll need to keep an eye on that. You don't want to get an injury like that infected."

The baby wailed.

"Sounds like he could use a good meal," Naomi remarked.

"I'll get him to the villa." Lydia scooped him up into her arms. "We always have goat's milk."

She thanked the midwife and promised to treat all the injuries as recommended.

Through the streets, Lydia rehearsed what she would say to James. She couldn't withhold the truth from him anymore, especially since she now had a baby to raise.

Inside the villa, Salome greeted her. "Sister!" She flew to her. "You're injured. What happened?"

"I'm well." Lydia pushed past her. "Where's James?"

"In the upper room."

"I've got to speak with him."

"He's talking with Nicolaus."

Lydia's foot stopped on the bottom step. Something inside her knew she was the topic of their conversation. She looked down into Stephen's face. "Salome?"

"Hmm?"

"Do me a favor." She turned around. "Get some

goat's milk, dip a cloth in it, and let this little one suck on it until he's had his fill." She held the babe out to her sister. "Then bring him back to me."

Salome accepted the bundle. "Who is he?"

"I'll tell you later." She looked up the stairs. "After I speak with James."

Salome moved toward the kitchen.

Lydia swallowed hard. She had a difficult discussion ahead of her, but she was thankful she'd only have to have it once. She cleared the stairs and entered the upper room.

James and Nicolaus sat at a low table, obviously deep in conversation.

"Sister?" James lifted. "Where have you been? What's on your head?"

Lydia's hand flew to the bump swelling on her forehead. "I have much to tell you." The ache in her arm returned. "May I sit?"

James waved to a nearby pillow.

Grateful, Lydia took it and recounted her tale for the two men. She began with the day of Stephen's stoning, told them about Reuben, her role in Penelope's death, and finally her discovery of the rock child now safe downstairs in Salome's arms.

Nicolaus flicked his gaze to James.

James leaned toward his sister. "But what of your injuries?"

"While seeking to rescue the child from his fate, a group of men surrounded me." Her breath shook. "They wanted to kill the babe, and I refused them. James," she looked into her brother's eyes, "Simon was among them."

"He did this?" James waved toward her.

"No." She shook her head. "The leader. But Simon injured the child."

James rose to his feet. "Did you recognize any of the others?"

"No." She dared a glance at Nicolaus. His typically olive complexion was a sickening green. "I only recognized Simon, but from his actions, I barely recognized our brother." Sobs threatened to steal her words as she dropped her gaze to the table.

James moved to exit the room.

"There's one more thing," Lydia said, not lifting her gaze.

"Speak," James demanded.

"I know why Nicolaus is here." She looked at the man. "I know he's here to ask your permission to marry me." She looked at James. "I want you both to know that I have every intention of raising the rock child as my own." She rose. "With or without a bridegroom."

Without allowing them any further say in the matter, Lydia left the two men to continue their discussion.

CHAPTER 26

The women of the villa provided for Lydia as they would a new mother, bringing her food and taking turns caring for the baby as she rested.

"Here." Elissa held out some folded material. "It's one of the ones your mother made for Joshua."

Lydia received the material. She recognized it as the same she purchased with Ria the day Saul had spoken such unkind things to her. Tears filled her eyes as she wrapped the baby in the soft cloth. The memory of Stephen's intervention washed over her. "May you be as brave as your name's sake, young one."

Elissa was the most involved in Lydia's care over the next few days. She shared her experiences and aided in newborn care. She even nursed baby Stephen to ease the supply of goat's milk.

In turn, Lydia shared the story of the fight with the men and how she rescued the baby from the rocks.

The two mothers spent their days talking while they cared for the two youngest family members.

Though Lydia's soul still drowned in sorrow, she was grateful that Elissa was equally content to listen as she was to speak. Her sister-in-law learned quickly when to ask questions and when to simply nurse Stephen and let Lydia sleep.

Naomi visited a few times to check on them and

provided fresh mixtures for their wounds. Between rest and Naomi's herbs, the cut on Lydia's hand began to heal and so did the rest of her physical injuries. The wound on the young one's thigh was closing without infection, but it would be a while before the extent of the deeper injury was fully known. The rest of his minor injuries faded within days.

By the last night of Joseph and Naavah's wedding feast, Lydia was bold enough to join the celebration. She cradled Stephen against her as she danced and introduced him to the others of the household. The women cooed over him, and the men remarked on his strong features.

While a slow song filled the air, a lone figure entered the room.

Lydia recognized the dirty gray cloak before anyone else. "Simon?"

Before he could step to her, James and Jude blocked his path.

"State your business," James ordered.

Simon bowed his head. "I've come to seek shelter."

"Why?"

"Brother, I've done terrible things." Simon glanced around James to catch sight of Lydia. "Things I'm no longer proud of, and I would like to confess something."

Jude leaned to whisper in James' ear. "Should we trust him?"

"Please?" Simon begged. "You must let me speak."

James gave a simple nod.

Simon pushed the hood of his cloak down. "I have

blood on my hands. More than I've ever wanted, but for the past few days, I've been running." He set pleading eyes on Lydia. "After the incident at the rocks, I couldn't return to my… group."

He cleared his throat. "I've hid among the shadows of Jerusalem. At first, I didn't know what I was searching for or even what I would do on my own." He spread his hands. "When I was hungry and tired, I cried out to Adonai. I must have passed out or something because all I remember is the man's voice. He gave me food and shared with me about Jesus."

Simon chuckled to himself. "He recounted lessons of my own brother. Stories I'd heard." He shook his head slowly. "I lived with Jesus my whole life, and it took me getting to my lowest and some stranger's kindness to have me realize the Truth." He looked at James. "I know Jesus is Messiah." Tears filled his eyes. "I know it with every part of me. I've asked for His forgiveness, but I need to ask for more."

He stepped toward Lydia, but James put up a hand to stop him.

"It's alright," Lydia said. "Let him come."

James dropped his hand.

Simon took a few cautious steps. "I can't begin to apologize for my role in everything that has happened." He took another step. "I never meant for you to get hurt. When I saw you on the ground—" His words caught in his throat. "It was one of the most sober moments I've had in a long time." He looked at the babe in her arms. "I hope you realize why I had to do what I did."

Lydia dropped her gaze to Stephen. It took only moments to hear the message behind his words. Her attention snapped to him. "You had to injure him to spare him."

Simon nodded. "I had to show them the blood on my dagger so they wouldn't return to do the deed themselves."

"You saved him." Lydia crushed Stephen against her chest. "Simon." She cleared the space between them and wrapped her brother with a free arm. "I knew you were still in there."

Simon buried his face in her hair. "It took you drawing me out." He stepped back. "And Jesus' forgiveness." His gaze traveled around the room. "And you." He moved toward Nicolaus. "You were the man who fed me."

"I was on my way to care for a widow when I saw you lying in the street. So many others passed you by, but I couldn't." Nicolaus turned to Lydia. "I kept thinking, 'What would Jesus and Stephen do?'" He lifted a shoulder. "They would have stopped to feed him, so I did."

James came closer. "I'm glad you have come to the Way, brother, but I don't think you can stay here. Saul is—"

"Hunting me," Simon finished. "I know." He looked around at them.

Lydia bit the inside of her cheek and rocked Stephen.

"It's true," Simon continued. "Saul is hunting me because of my part in Penelope's death. He's also seeking vengeance on the rest of my family and all Way Followers."

"The council has agreed to his war," James added.

"This isn't war, brother." Simon put a hand on James' shoulder. "War has rules. This is hunting."

"What can we do?"

Simon dropped his hand. "The only choice prey has; hide or be eaten."

"Saul is making it impossible to hide in Jerusalem." James shook his head.

"Then we must flee," Simon suggested.

"Where?" James asked. "We have so many here in Jerusalem who depend on us. Widows. New believers. We can't just abandon them."

"We can't stay together. It's too dangerous."

"At least Saul seems content to hunt within the city. Assia is safe in Nazareth."

"Saul is a hungry predator," Simon reminded him. "I don't think his hunting grounds will remain contained for long. Especially not when the Way is spreading beyond Jerusalem. His hunger will not be satisfied until he has captured every last one of us. Mark my words."

"Should we send you to Nazareth?" James asked.

Simon looked at Lydia.

She gulped.

"No," Simon answered. "I don't want to draw attention to our family there."

"What about Damascus?" Lydia offered.

"We have friends there," James explained. "Fellow Way Followers who might hide you until we can deal with Saul." He looked at Lydia. "If nothing else, at least Simon will be able to warn Ananias about what's happening. He might be the one to provide us with aid this time."

Simon gazed around the gathering. "What about Ima and the girls?"

Mary stepped forward. "I'm staying with John."

"Ima." James groaned.

"Jesus put John in charge of me for good reason." Mary folded her arms. "I have to keep my faith in His choice."

Simon turned to their youngest sister. "Salome?"

"I can send her back to Nazareth," James answered for her.

Lydia chuckled. "I'd think you'd have an easier time commanding the waves. Ever since that fiery tongue licked her head, she's been an unstoppable sandstorm. I don't think you could make her do anything, even if you tied her to a camel." She glanced in Salome's direction.

"Saul doesn't scare me," Salome announced. "My big brother can handle him."

Lydia smiled. *If only we all had that much faith.*

"And you?" Simon asked, looking down at the baby in Lydia's arms.

Lydia set her gaze on each of her siblings, then she shifted her eyes to Nicolaus. "I have an offer of marriage." She inclined her head toward him. "If he's willing to take a widow and an orphan as his own, I will go where he leads."

CHAPTER 27

The following morning, Lydia stood among as many believers who dared gather to hear Peter share a lesson. Tears of bittersweet joy washed her face as she soaked in the last time she would worship in Jerusalem among her brother's followers. People who had become as close as her siblings circled her. She felt their warmth and their love as they sang praises to Adonai.

After Peter's last prayer, Lydia followed her family to Rabbi Ethan's synagogue.

"I know it's all so sudden," she explained to Ethan, "but with everything happening right now, we think it best."

"I agree," Ethan said with a raised silver eyebrow. "It is outside of tradition. You haven't even completed your year of mourning."

Lydia carefully moved baby Stephen into Salome's arms. "We wouldn't be asking you to perform these ceremonies if it wasn't urgent."

"I should say so." He tucked his hands into the folds of his tunic. "You want me to perform a betrothal agreement, a circumcision, and a wedding all together?"

"Please?" She put her hands together. "Stephen would understand."

"Well," he smiled, "what are we waiting for?"

Lydia kissed his cheek. "Bless you, Rabbi."

Standing in her widow's garment, Lydia exchanged promises and gifts with Nicolaus in the form of a shortened betrothal agreement. She wanted to share these moments with her family and Nicolaus, even though the completion of the promise would quickly follow the ceremony.

Once they signed the parchments, Lydia retrieved baby Stephen from Salome. She escorted her son to Nicolaus and watched the rabbi tenderly perform a circumcision and welcome the boy into the fold of Abraham.

With baby Stephen's pitiful cries as a replacement for instruments, Lydia placed him safely back into Salome's arms so she could join Nicolaus' side.

He turned toward her. "This part can wait until we arrive in Antioch." He looked around the room. "We don't have to rush everything."

Lydia followed his gaze. "I want to be wed in the presence of my family." Her eyes returned to his. "It might be a long time before we are all together again."

"If it is your desire." Nicolaus stepped toward James. "I ask for your sister, Lydia, to be my wife," he said formally. "She is my wife, and I am her husband from this day and forever."

James took Lydia's hands into one of his and placed his other over hers. With lips moving in silent prayers, he patted her hands. When he finished, he extended Lydia's hands toward Nicolaus. "She is yours."

Nicolaus' warm hands enveloped hers as she was passed from brother to bridegroom.

Ethan offered a cup of wine, allowing Nicolaus and Lydia to each take a sip from it.

The small gathering lifted shouts of praise and passed the couple from arms to arms.

"Sorry we don't have time for a feast," Lydia apologized to Salome as she accepted Stephen back into her aching arms. "Nicolaus has a caravan waiting for us."

"We understand." Salome kissed baby Stephen's forehead.

Nicolaus came to her side. "Ready?"

"I have one last request before we leave for Antioch."

"What is it?"

"It's back at the villa."

Lydia made her way slowly through the streets of Jerusalem. Her feet ached with longing to return to the place before they had even left. Something inside told her these would be her last moments in the holy city.

Inside the villa, she allowed Salome to hold baby Stephen while she took time to speak to Zipporah and Ria, the two women beside whom she spent many of her days. She also spoke blessings over each woman who'd come from Galilee, begging Adonai for their protection. She collected her meager possessions from the room she shared with her mother and sisters and found her way downstairs.

"You're forgetting one last thing." Mary came toward her, holding a folded blue dress. "I did what I could."

Lydia unfolded the garment to discover that every

stain had been removed. "It's perfect." She fingered the tear at the shoulder and sighed. "I wish I hadn't ripped the only dress that was ever only mine. It would go against our custom to repair it."

"One day all the tears of this life will be mended. Until then," Mary embraced her daughter, "may Adonai make His face shine upon you and keep you."

Tears burned her eyes. "I will miss you, Ima. Thank you. For everything." She looked to Salome. "I will miss you as well, sister."

Salome kissed Stephen's head and extended him out to Lydia. "I can't believe Adonai is taking you away, too."

"He's not taking us away," Lydia corrected. "He's moving me where I'm supposed to be." She winked. "He's got you where He wants you, too." She took Stephen into her arms.

Elissa held Joshua on her hip. "Now remember what we talked about concerning Stephen's circumcision. You'll need to keep an eye on it."

Lydia smiled. "I will."

"And remember to keep up with his feedings." She wiped at her face. "He's a growing boy and will need more and more milk before he can try anything else."

Lydia kissed her sister-in-law's cheek and let out a chuckle. "I'll remember." She turned to Nicolaus. "Just one more thing."

With slow steps, Lydia took Stephen to the outer courtyard.

The chickens scurried around her feet as her sandals stirred the grass and bugs. Jacob and Esau bounded around her with their little leaps and cries. Michal and Abigail munched on the grass beside Daniel.

Lydia's heart swelled as she stepped into her place of comfort. Her chief desire was to express gratitude to the creatures who had made her lowest days tolerable.

"I'm sorry you all won't get to see Stephen grow." She paced around the open space. "I so wish I could take you all with me." She moved toward the overhang where Boaz and Judith lay among the straw.

Boaz rose and softly nuzzled her arm.

Lydia reached over to brush his long nose. "Theodotus agreed to let us take you," she whispered. "It seems only fitting that I care for the donkey who ushered in our King." She turned to his mother. "I promise to take good care of him, Judith."

The mother donkey brayed at her in response.

"Kraa."

The sudden noise caused Stephen to let out a cry of displeasure.

Lydia saw Elijah dance on the wooden rail. She soothed Stephen with gentle coos. "This is my friend, Elijah, that I've shared so much about." She moved him toward the bird.

Elijah hopped closer and tilted his head toward the baby. "He'll be well. You just frightened him."

Stephen quieted down.

"I will miss you." Lydia stroked Elijah's gray body. "Take care of the others and watch over my siblings for me."

Elijah flapped his wings and answered, "Kraa-

kraa."

Lydia sighed. "I will miss you most of all, my friend." She turned back toward the collection of animals. "I will miss you all more than I can express, but I know I'm going where Adonai wants me."

She looked down at the babe in her arms.

A flash of ginger shone up at her.

The words of David's psalm came to her. She parted her lips and sang the verse she couldn't finish the day of Stephen's stoning, "But I have trusted in Your steadfast love; my heart shall rejoice in Your salvation. I will sing to the Lord, because He has dealt bountifully with me." She hummed the song over baby Stephen.

Nicolaus stepped into the courtyard. "Ready?" He held two ropes in his hands.

"I'm not sure I'll ever be ready to leave my friends." She waved around the space. "And my family, and my friends, and... Stephen."

With a steady stride, Nicolaus came toward her. "We are only leaving Stephen's body here in Jerusalem." He moved to rope the young donkey. "We will carry his memories with us." He handed her the rope to lead Boaz, kissed baby Stephen's head, then asked, "Which one's Michal?"

"That one." Lydia pointed to the female goats.

Nicolaus secured the second lead over Michal's head. "We'll need a lot of goat's milk for young Stephen."

She looked between Boaz and Michal. "I'm so thankful Theodotus is willing to part with these two."

"I am as well." Nicolaus scratched behind Michal's ear.

Lydia's insides fluttered at his kindness. *Thank you for choosing him, Stephen.* She moved toward her husband. "When we get to Antioch, we shall share of all Stephen did in Jesus' name and keep his memory alive for all those who follow the Way."

Nicolaus nodded and led Michal out of the courtyard.

Lydia trailed behind him with her rock baby in her arms and Boaz following behind. In her heart, she knew that even though Stephen was standing with her brother in the heavens, a small piece of him would be carried with her to Antioch. A piece of her beloved would be with her until she once again looked into those bright ginger eyes.

What's Next?

What will peace cost?

Simon wanted nothing more than for his dagger to taste Roman blood. With his father's untimely death and a house full of siblings, his plans to join the rebellion against Rome were traded for endless days of hard labor.

When his older brother, Jesus, began teaching extremist ideas, Simon's hopes for the removal of Rome and the establishment of a true nation of Israel were sparked once again. Simon would have been happy to follow Jesus as a warrior-king like their ancestor, but his brother chose the path of martyrdom.

Discontent with his Messiah-brother's sacrifice, Simon disappeared to join the Zealots and fight for the freedom promised to the chosen people.

While entrenched in the tactics of zealous warfare, Simon discovers that fighting for peace may cost him more than he's willing to pay. Will he shed innocent blood to bring down Rome?

Dive deep into the historical beginnings of the early church in *Simon*, book 6 of the Servant Siblings series.

More from Jenifer Jennings:

Special Collections and Boxed Sets
Biblical Historical stories from the Old Testament to the New, these special boxed editions offer a great way to catch up or to fall in love with Jenifer Jennings' books for the first time.

The Rebekah Series: Books 1-3
Faith Finder Series: Books 1-3
Faith Finders Series: Books 4-6
Servant Siblings Series: Books 1-3
Servant Siblings Series: Books 4-7
Paul's Patrons Series: Books 1-3
Paul's Patrons Series: Books 4-6

* * *

The Rebekah Series:
Follow Rebekah on her faith journey from the fields of her homeland to being part of Abraham's family.

The Stranger
The Journey
The Hope

* * *

Faith Finders Series:

Go deeper into the stories of these familiar faith heroines.

Midwives of Moses
Wilderness Wanderer
Crimson Cord
A Stolen Wife
At His Feet
Lasting Legacy

* * *

Servant Siblings Series:

*They were Jesus' siblings,
but they become His followers.*

James
Joseph
Assia
Jude
Lydia
Simon
Salome

* * *

Paul's Patrons Series:

Little-known supporters of Paul's ministry have their own stories to tell.

Leading Philippi
Keeping Thessalonica
Warring Corinth
Serving Rome
Finding Colossae
Tending Crete

Find these titles at your favorite retailer or at:
jeniferjennings.com/books

* * *

If this story inspired you, consider sharing your honest thoughts in a review. Your words help spread these stories of faith even further.

About the Author

Jenifer Jennings is a passionate storyteller who brings ancient worlds to life through Biblical historical novels. A devoted student of Scripture since coming to faith in Jesus at seventeen, she holds a bachelor's degree in Women's Ministry and a master's in Biblical Languages. Jenifer is an active member of Word Weavers International, serving as an online chapter president, and a member of American Christian Fiction Writers (ACFW). When Jenifer's not writing, she's on a date with her husband or mothering their two children, a wise-cracking mathematician and a feisty artist.

If you'd like to keep up with new releases, receive spiritual encouragement, and get your hands on a FREE book, then join Jenifer's Newsletter at:
jeniferjennings.com/gift

www.ingramcontent.com/pod-product-compliance
Lightning Source LLC
Chambersburg PA
CBHW060932180626
46817CB00004B/1506